THE
DOUBLE TURN

THE DOUBLE TURN

Carol Carnac

with an introduction by
MARTIN EDWARDS

This edition first published in 2026 by
The British Library
96 Euston Road
London NW1 2DB
bl.uk

1 3 5 7 9 10 8 6 4 2

The Double Turn was first published in 1956
by Collins Crime Club, London.

Introduction © 2026 Martin Edwards
The Double Turn © 1956 The Estate of Carol Carnac
Volume copyright © 2026 The British Library Board

Represented in the EU by Authorised Rep Compliance
Ltd., Ground Floor, 71 Lower Baggot Street, Dublin,
D02 P593, Ireland. arccompliance.com

Cataloguing in Publication Data
A catalogue record for this publication is
available from the British Library

ISBN 978 0 7123 6900 8
e-ISBN 978 0 7123 6270 2

Cover Illustration © Herbert Art Gallery &
Museum, Coventry / Bridgeman Images
Text design and typesetting by Tetragon, London
Printed in England by CPI Group (UK) Ltd, Croydon, CR0 4YY

CONTENTS

Introduction   7
A Note from the Publisher   11

THE DOUBLE TURN   13

INTRODUCTION

The Double Turn, first published in 1956, opens at an exhibition of Victorian art in the long gallery of Verulam House in London. Jocelyn Truby, his attractive young niece Susan Truby, and her admirer Peter Raven contemplate a vast canvas which was the first success for the once-renowned artist Adrian Delafield and was exhibited at the Royal Academy.

The presence of his work prompts a conversation about Delafield. Jocelyn explains that the elderly painter is still alive, although weakened by a stroke that affected his eyesight and caused him to stop work. The two men were acquainted at one time and Susan is interested in what Jocelyn has to say about Delafield. A would-be artist herself, she is researching Victorian painters and wants "to get a line on famous academicians of fifty years ago: how they lived, what their houses were like, what they really thought of these enormous objects we've been looking at."

Another young man, who was in the army with Peter, joins the group and turns out to be Adrian Delafield's grandson. This is Roy Braithwaite, and to Peter's dismay he quickly takes an interest in Susan. Adrian Delafield, it turns out, lives in a house called "Firenze" in St. John's Wood, and Roy invites Susan to see it for herself: "It's quite an exhibit. The old boy's studio is still pasted over with his throw-outs—they didn't all sell."

Roy offers to show her the studio, which has now been taken over by his Aunt Virgilia, but explains that actually, a woman called Trimming "runs that house more or less single-handed, tyrannises over the Ancient, feeds him, nurses him, dresses him. Trimming's a terror, but she keeps the wheels turning." As for Adrian Delafield, sometimes he is "gaga", but at other times "he's quite on the spot and very picturesque in a bygone manner." He is, however, a recluse, and Miss Trimming keeps him in seclusion: "She overdid it at one time and the rumour went round that he didn't really exist, because no one ever saw him." Jocelyn remembers Miss Trimming as a wonderful cook, but in the grip of religion: "A very severe and virtuous woman… She looked like a deaconess."

Susan learns that Roy works as a courier and wonders if there might be a job for her in the same field, since she isn't getting anywhere with her own painting and is desperate not to end up as a typist like so many of her old schoolfriends. When the party breaks up, Jocelyn continues talking to Roy, and discovers that Adrian Delafield is living on an annuity, so is unable to give his grandson financial help with his business plans. Roy invites Jocelyn to "Firenze", but warns him that it's "a very odd set-up."

In the studio, Virgilia—a Cambridge-educated academic and writer—talks to Adrian's new doctor about the old man's health and is assured that Adrian is remarkably fit for his age. They also discuss Miss Trimming, whom Virgilia regards as "quite mad" but "very shrewd." In her opinion, Miss Trimming has religious mania and "regards my father as her own possession." But Adrian has depended on her for thirty-five years and refuses to sack her. Virgilia has even wondered if Miss Trimming might murder her, although she thinks it more likely that the woman would take her own life.

When Jocelyn visits "Firenze", he is introduced by Virgilia to Miss Trimming, and she in turn takes him to see Adrian Delafield. At this point, Virgilia suffers a minor accident, being hit on the head by a board that has become dislodged. A plasterer has been working in the house and Virgilia's mishap is blamed on him. But the strangeness of the household disturbs Jocelyn. And the next development is that Miss Trimming is found dead...

This novel, published under the pen name Carol Carnac, appeared in Britain under the Collins Crime Club imprint; the American edition, which appeared in 1957, was given a new title, *The Late Miss Trimming*. This is the only Carol Carnac story to feature in the late Bob Adey's magisterial reference book *Locked Room Murders*: the central problem is the cause of death, by a broken neck, in a locked house. But Carnac was a very different writer from, say, John Dickson Carr. Her interest lies less in the technicalities of howdunit (and even, dare I say it, the question of whodunit) than in the interplay of character and setting. This fascination with what we now call "human geography" is a strand that runs through all her writing, from the earliest novels right to the end of her life.

The stern American critics Jacques Barzun and Wendell Hertig Taylor praised the book in their highly informative (and highly opinionated) reference book *A Catalogue of Crime*: "A did-she-fall-or-was-she-pushed? tale, with interesting characterisation and better-than-average psychological clueing-in of the right suspects."

Carol Carnac was a pen name of Edith Caroline Rivett (1894–1958) who is better known under another pseudonym, E. C. R. Lorac. This novel is distinctive, yet typical of her best work. She was familiar with the London setting: the sixth Lorac novel was *Murder in St. John's Wood* (1934). A talented artist, she was fascinated by the art world, and this book (like *Murder as a Fine Art*, a Carnac novel published three years earlier than this one, and also reprinted as a British Library Crime Classic) gave her a platform to express her opinions about art. And her scathing depiction of the deceased's religious mania reflects a distaste for excessive, and often hypocritical, piety to be found in several of her books.

The Lorac books were, in their day, better known and (to generalise) better regarded by the critics than the Carnac titles, but the British Library's republication of several of Inspector Rivers' cases, starting with *Crossed Skis*, has demonstrated that there is no shortage of hidden gems in her output. She died just two years after *The Double Turn* first appeared, but here as in other books of the 1950s, there is no sense that this prolific author was tiring or running out of ideas. Rather, she had developed full confidence in her own ability to keep readers interested, a crucial advantage for any author so long as it isn't misplaced. The remarkable success that her fiction has enjoyed in recent years thanks to the Crime Classics series is testament to the fact that her faith in herself was justified.

MARTIN EDWARDS
www.martinedwardsbooks.com

A NOTE FROM THE PUBLISHER

The original novels and short stories reprinted in the British Library Crime Classics series were written and published in a period ranging, for the most part, from the 1890s to the 1960s. There are many elements of these stories which continue to entertain modern readers; however, in some cases there are also uses of language, instances of stereotyping and some attitudes expressed by narrators or characters which may not be endorsed by the publishing standards of today. We acknowledge therefore that some elements in the works selected for reprinting may continue to make uncomfortable reading for some of our audience. With this series British Library Publishing aims to offer a new readership a chance to read some of the rare books of the British Library's collections in an affordable paperback format, to enjoy their merits and to look back into the world of the twentieth century as portrayed by its writers. It is not possible to separate these stories from the history of their writing and therefore the following novel is presented as it was originally published with one edit to the text, and minor edits made for consistency of style and sense. We welcome feedback from our readers, which can be sent to the following address:

> British Library Publishing
> The British Library
> 96 Euston Road
> London, NW1 2DB
> United Kingdom

THE DOUBLE TURN

I

I

"DEAD? NOTHING OF THE KIND, MY DEAR. HE'S STILL alive, very much alive," said Jocelyn Truby. He glanced up at the huge canvas again and then added testily: "The trouble with you youngsters of to-day is that you're so contemporary-minded you tend to think of the Victorians as ancient history, on a par with Alfred and the cakes. I'm a Victorian myself, and proud of it. I can remember her funeral—and I'm still *compos mentis*."

Susan Truby tucked her arm in her uncle's and spoke apologetically. "It's one thing to remember Victoria's funeral, Jocelyn, dear"—he *was* a dear, too, she thought to herself—"and it's quite another to be a Great Victorian. The catalogue says this object was painted in 1897. Gosh, that's the last century!"

"Yes, it is, and I was born in it," said Jocelyn firmly, "and I'm still going strong. Adrian Delafield was born in 1870. This picture was his first big success. It was shown in the Academy of 1898. My father and mother went to see it."

"It is big, isn't it?" murmured Susan. "They did rather run to size in those days; fancy having that canvas in the drawing-room."

"It wasn't painted for a drawing-room," said Jocelyn firmly. "It was bought by one of the provincial galleries—Bromcaster—and very proud of it they were. Felt one up on Liverpool."

"It's not Art in any sense," put in Peter Raven firmly. "It's pure narrative, story book stuff, like 'The Boyhood of Raleigh' and The Doctor,' if you happen to remember that one."

"Remember it? Of course I do," said Jocelyn Truby. "Luke Fildes—his greatest picture. I believe one of the northern medical schools commissioned a copy of it."

"And they got paid enormous sums for the things, didn't they?" said Susan pensively. Susan painted herself, but nobody ever bought her pictures.

"Enormous," echoed Peter. He was a very tall young man, and his height seemed to add weight to his pronouncements. "They made fortunes. Look at the houses they built themselves— Leighton, Alma Tadema, McWhirter. They were paid thousands for these monstrosities and income tax was ninepence in the pound."

"It does seem a bit hard," said Susan. "Hard on us, I mean. Not that I'd mind income tax at whatever it is if I could make an income."

"Come and have some tea, my dear," said Jocelyn. "Nothing more tiring than looking at pictures—though I've enjoyed this, by jove I have! And there's old Herkomer's 'Duchess'—there's a figure for you…"

"How did they *do* it?" asked Susan weakly, and Peter replied:

"You should read *The Edwardians*—Sackville West. She *tells* you how they did it, chapter and verse, corsets and pads…"

The exhibition to which Jocelyn Truby had brought his niece (Peter had tagged on to the party because of Susan) was held in the long gallery of Verulam House: it was sponsored by the Central Arts Committee, and was in aid of aged and indigent painters. The exhibition consisted of English pictures painted between 1890 and 1910, and it was being a great success. Large numbers of "fools who came to scoff" (though none remained to pray) paid their half-crowns gladly for the enjoyment of a good laugh at what once passed for painting. Older folks thronged to see the pictorial sensations of their youth—the "problem" picture, the historic masterpiece, the battle picture, the civic commemoration: "Cheats" and Joans of Arc, happy warriors and bechained aldermen crowded the walls in exuberant realism, every detail faithful to the last card in the pack, gleam on the blade, quartering of escutcheon. As Susan said, "They did take trouble in those days..." Seated at tea (a very good tea, too, provided by a thoughtful committee at five shillings a head), Susan poured out sedately.

"You're giving us a lovely afternoon, Jocelyn, dear. This tea is simply superb—tomato sandwiches, and cucumber—everything I like best." She paused, and then added: "I do wish you'd tell me about Adrian Delafield. Does he still paint?"

"No. Not since he had a slight stroke which affected his eyesight—just after the end of the war, that was. But he was exhibiting in the thirties, and selling his pictures, too. Some of the Dominion galleries still paid good prices for his stuff—and commissioned it, too. Historical subjects mainly, sometimes with a Colonial flavour. But the time for big prices was the early nineteen hundreds. Popular painters made enormous prices then: they really were rich men—as some of the film stars are to-day."

Peter Raven grinned. "Ephemerals?" he murmured. "Who will last longest, the popular academician or the early film star?"

"Who cares?" said Susan, bending forward to see if her uncle's cup needed refilling—she was a mannerly young woman. "Is Adrian still rich, and did he build himself a house?"

"So far as I know, he's still a very prosperous old gentleman," replied Jocelyn. "I knew him at one time: we commissioned him to paint 'The Glorious Tenth' for our Regimental Mess. 1919, that was. After the battalion was disbanded we gave the picture to the War Museum..." He chuckled and his blue eyes smiled at Susan. "Ancient history, miss. Why are you interested in Delafield?"

"Because you knew him," she replied. "I want to get a line on the famous academicians of fifty years ago: how they lived, what their houses were like, what they really thought of these enormous objects we've been looking at." She smiled at Jocelyn Truby in her turn, and he thought how lovely she was: so young, so serious in her inquiries.

"You see, they're mostly dead," she went on. "Tadema, with his marbles, and McWhirter with his highland mists, and Poynter with his Grecian youths and John Collier with his Sentences of Death. It all seems such a long time ago to me—"

"'Old unhappy far-off things and battles long ago,'" quoted Peter flippantly, and Susan snapped back at him:

"Don't interrupt—and they weren't unhappy, anyway. They were terribly sure of everything and awfully pleased with themselves. I want to know if the surviving ones are still pleased, or if a doubt has ever percolated. And you say Adrian Delafield is still alive," she added to Jocelyn.

"He must be. *The Times* would certainly have spared him an inch—possibly two inches," replied Truby. "One of the few topics of to-day I'm reliable on is obituaries. I always read them." He passed his cup across to Susan, and went on: "Delafield didn't build himself a house. He bought old Solly Barnato's house in St. John's Wood, when Solly went bankrupt for the third time. It's a nice house—Regency and slightly rococo. Delafield built himself a studio in the garden and planted a cypress walk."

"Cypresses—in St. John's Wood? Are they still there?" asked Susan.

"I expect so," replied Truby. "I haven't been that way for a long time, but I'm pretty certain old Delafield's still living in Firenze. He called it that when he moved in. He was an admirer of Ruskin."

"'Stones of Tuscany,'" murmured Susan. "Or was it Venice?..."

"Likewise Sesame and Lilies and Modern Painters," put in Peter loftily. "Hallo, what brings you here?"

Another young man had halted beside the table, after a sidelong glance at Susan which Peter had noted. Peter was tall and dark, the newcomer short (in comparison with Peter's six foot three) and fair—but a personable young man. He replied to Peter's query.

"Grandfilial piety. I came to see some of the Ancient's more famous efforts. I'm his grandson—Adrian Delafield's, I mean."

"But how marvellous!" exclaimed Susan. (She had black hair and blue eyes and used both to advantage.) "I've just been asking my uncle about Adrian Delafield. That 'Phillippa of Hainault' thing of his is terrific."

A thought belatedly, making a virtue of necessity, Peter introduced the newcomer. "Roy Braithwaite—we were in the army together. Miss Truby, Mr. Truby."

"Braithwaite," echoed Jocelyn with satisfaction. "You'll be Mifanwy's son. I think I met her in 1919. Delighted to meet you. Come and have tea and answer Susan's questions. She's intent on researching into the Victorian painters."

Susan smiled and moved her chair so that Roy could sit between her and Peter.

"Mifanwy," she murmured, and Roy smiled back.

"It was the old man's Celtic period," he said. "My mother said it only lasted until the Academy turned down his 'Harpist of the Mists.' She called herself Milly in self-defence."

"I never heard that you were Delafield's grandson," said Peter huffily.

"Not the sort of thing one brags about," said Roy; "but it's true. Of course I didn't see the Ancient in his prime: he was about sixty when I put in an appearance, but he was still pretty active. He'd cover an acre or so of canvas in record time even then."

"Are the cypresses still there?" asked Susan.

Roy had no difficulty in switching to this one. "Some of them, but they're pretty moth-eaten. I don't think they like St. John's Wood. Look here; if you're really interested, why not come and see the place? It's quite an exhibit. The old boy's studio is still pasted over with his throw-outs—they didn't all sell. They're incredible, they are really. I know I can show you the studio because Aunt Virgilia's taken it over. She's quite affable and it's not her fault she was called Virgilia."

"She was the intellectual of the family," said Jocelyn; "went to Girton and read History. Never married, did she? There were Mifanwy and Virgilia and Sandro."

"That's right, sir," said Roy. "Sandro was killed in the 1914–1918 to-do: and my mater died in 1940, so Virgilia's the only one left of that generation. She's still the intellectual, writes mighty tomes on hitherto un-elucidated historical minutiæ. Did you ever know Trimming?"

"Trimming?" echoed Jocelyn. "Was she the cook? I seem to remember the name."

"Trimming is the boss: the power in the house," said Roy. "She is the *ménagère* and major-domo. She still runs that house more or less single-handed, tyrannises over the Ancient, feeds him, nurses him, dresses him. Trimming's a terror, but she keeps the wheels turning. When Auntie V. turned up and said she was going to live in the studio and keep an eye on things, there was war to the knife—but Auntie V. won. It's a wonderful household."

"Is the old man—?" Jocelyn hesitated, and Roy put in cheerfully:

"Gaga? Some days he is. Other's he's quite on the spot and very picturesque in a bygone manner. He's a recluse, of course, with a capital R. Trimming sees to that. At one time she kept him so secluded—could one say re-cluded—?"

"No. One could not," said Peter coldly.

"All right. He's a recluse, kept in seclusion by Trimming. She overdid it at one time and the rumour went round that he didn't really exist, because no one ever saw him. Auntie V. butted in when she heard that one and insisted on a—what is it?"

"Habeas Corpus?" suggested Susan, and Roy grinned at her happily.

"Got it in one. In other words, the doctor was told to come every week and look the Ancient over, and a minister of Trimming's variety of religion comes once a month and they have the equivalent of a prayer party. I must say it seems to work, because the Ancient's very spry. He even walks in the garden on summer evenings."

"In the cypress walk?" asked Susan sympathetically. "All Tennysonian?"

"Yes, exactly like that," agreed Roy.

"Trimming," said Jocelyn in a gratified voice. "It's coming back. I heard your grandfather talk about her: it must have been in 1920, so Trimming's no chicken. She was a wonderful cook, but she had religion. A very severe and virtuous young woman who wore a long black frock and a black apron and a comprehensive cap. I only caught a glimpse of her once. She looked like a deaconess."

"She still does," said Roy. "She hasn't altered all my life, not a hair. Although you can't see her hair because she affects a veil these days—nun-like. '... Breathless with adoration,' you know. She has a cult, and the Ancient is the cult."

"It sounds marvellous," said Susan. "Much, *much* better than I hoped for when I got Jocelyn to open up. I was thinking in terms of a frock-coat and Gladstone collar, with Lord Leightonish hair and a gold albert in front. I never dreamt of a breathless deaconess."

"He never belonged to the frock-coated school," said Roy. "He was a painter of the Bohemian period. Velvet jacket, flowing tie and baggy bags. And he has an imperial: it's a bit frazzled now, but very neatly trimmed."

"By Trimming?" inquired Peter, and Susan giggled.

"It sounds wonderful. Is she really devout?"

"She is indeed," said Roy. "I don't know the precise brand or sect, but something ultra-pi and Protestant. I believe she still thinks of Scarlet Women and papist abominations. Her sect is very strict and negative: it's all don'ts. I know that because I was always don'ted vigorously when I was taken there to tea at the age of six—but she understood about teas."

"The age of innocence," said Peter, with a hostile gleam in his eye. "Did grandpapa paint you, all dolled up in a velvet suit?"

"Actually, he did paint me," said Roy serenely; "but you've got your periods muddled. I was six when you were six and I was no more velveteened than you were. It's true my mamma was rather elderly when I happened, but she was sensible. She never put me in fancy dress. The Ancient said I was an uncompromising subject. I remember him saying it and I thought it meant the equivalent of bloody."

"What happened to the portrait?" asked Susan sympathetically.

"It went in the blitz—all our things did. Direct hit. Mother and all."

He spoke with the calm of those who were still young when "blitz" was a newly-coined word, and Jocelyn asked suddenly: "How old are you?"

"Twenty-eight, sir. I was thirteen when that happened—evacuated, you know. It all seems such a long time ago and such a lot of things happened at once that one got rather pachydermatous."

"You had a brother?" asked Jocelyn.

"Yes. Adrian. He was ten years older than I was and didn't think much of me. I suppose he didn't like an infant happening when he'd been the only pebble on the beach so long. Anyway, he was pilot in one of our aircraft which didn't return, you know. Sorry to give such a list of family casualties, but it just happened like that."

"So apart from Virgilia, you're the only descendant of Adrian Delafield," said Jocelyn, and Roy replied:

"I suppose I am—though, I don't really know."

"Do you paint yourself?" asked Susan.

"No. I've never dared—in case somebody connected me with the Ancient," said Roy, but Peter put in rather aggressively:

"Weren't you painting with that chap who did frescoes, in the Cologne barracks? You covered enough surface with dotty pictures—or don't you call that painting?"

"I call it house painting—quite a different thing," said Roy.

"What was his name—the fresco chap—De Fraine? He was a good painter—and not much else."

"Sez you—being the authority," mocked Roy, and turned to Susan again. "I'm a courier," he said. "Coaches and things. Cultural tours."

"Gosh!" said Susan. "You mean you ride in the front and have a mike and give pep talks to tourists? 'We are now approaching the city of Florence. On your right the campanile soars heavenwards...' That sort of thing?"

"More or less," he admitted, "though I'm not tied to a script. Improvising for a mixed selection of morons has its diverting side."

"God!" said Peter. "A courier... Why on earth?"

"Because I choose," said Roy. "I find it more palatable than being bound to a government department and writing minutes on statistics. *Chacun à son métier*—you to your small world and me to mine."

"Modern languages," put in Jocelyn. "You were brought up on the Continent, weren't you?"

"Yes, sir. That's the idea. I speak French and German and Italian, and I like going places and seeing things. Couriering seemed preferable to teaching—or minute-mongering."

Susan laughed. "I think you're rather enterprising. Is there any scope for females of the species? I'm not getting anywhere with painting, and it's my abiding fear that I shall eventually get tied to a typewriter. Nearly all the girls I was at school with have gone the same road."

"Typing is the last infirmity of conditioned minds," said Roy, and Jocelyn looked round for his hat. It seemed to him that the two young men were heading for mutual insults, and Jocelyn was a peaceful character.

"I must be getting home, my dear," he said to Susan. "I've got to write my weekly letter to Di—I always write to her on Monday evening, and I shall be able to tell her about this show. I'll send her the catalogue—she'll be delighted. She saw most of these exhibits in the Academy shows of fifty years ago."

"Give Aunt Di my love and tell her how much I enjoyed it," said Susan. "And thank you again, Jocelyn. It's been a lovely afternoon."

"Bless you," said her uncle. "You've always been a charming child to take out. Come and see me some time and we'll talk over that trip to Rome you've set your heart on. Now I know you want to hurry off, so I'll say good-bye. Have a good time!"

2

Susan went off with Peter (who had organised a party for her), and old Jocelyn Truby found himself left with Roy Braithwaite. With a quizzical glance Jocelyn inquired:

"Rome? Is that in your line?"

"Yes, sir. Definitely," said Roy. "I can tell you every possible way of reaching Rome, including comparative costs, comparative advantages—and of course disadvantages. And where to stay and not to stay."

"Well, that might be helpful," said Jocelyn. "I propose to walk up Bond Street. May I assume that you still have the use of your legs, or do you belong to the immobilised-without-a-car school?"

Roy laughed. "I'm a pedestrian, sir, on principle. Natural reaction to coaches. I haven't got a car. I've never had one."

"Delighted to hear it," said Jocelyn as they turned towards Bond Street. "Now I know nothing of this conducted tour business."

"Well, sir, it may not be good business to say so, but if you're asking my advice, I say—don't. It's not your cup of tea, nor Miss Truby's either."

"I rather suspected it," replied Truby, "but what'd your bosses say if they heard you crabbing their methods?"

"I haven't a boss at the moment. I've just finished my three years' contract with Universitas—and I've learnt a lot, which was what I went into it for. I'm hoping to start my own concern sometime—but that's only an aspiration at the moment."

"Like everything else, needs capital," said Truby, and switched the conversation back to the subject which really interested him. "Would your grandfather help?"

"Not he," said Roy promptly, "and he hasn't got any capital, anyway."

"You surprise me," said Jocelyn Truby.

"He lost his nerve and put it all into an annuity," said Roy. "Auntie V. know about it. The consequence is he's very cosy on the proceeds, and as he's obviously going to emulate Methusalah, the company which took him on may have cause to regret it."

Jocelyn Truby chuckled. "I wish him luck—and longevity. But that doesn't help you, does it? He was a remarkable old chap: even when I knew him he was assuming the privileges of the oldest inhabitant, so to speak."

"I sometimes wish I knew more about him," said Roy. "My mother used to hint that he'd been a lively sinner in his time, but I never got her to give chapter and verse. Look here, sir: if you'd really like to see the old man again, why not come and see Auntie V. in the studio? I'd fix it up, and she'd take you along in to see him."

"Frankly, I should be most interested," said Mr. Truby. "I'll give you my card. I'm generally free in the afternoons—retired from active service, you know. And we might have a word about this Rome trip. If you know the ropes you could give some professional advice. I haven't been in Rome since 1925 and I dare say things have changed a bit since then."

"Quite a bit," agreed Roy, and Jocelyn Truby asked abruptly:

"I wonder if Trimming knows about the annuity? These ultra-devout bodies often have an eye on the future."

Roy laughed out loud. "How right you are, sir. I always think Trimming keeps her eyes on the immediate future as well as on mansions in the skies. But if you ask me, the Ancient's still much too cunning to let Trimming know more than's good for her. But come along and give the household the once-over. It's quite an experience."

"I won't say no," said Mr. Truby. "You're not living there yourself, are you?"

"My God, no!" exclaimed Roy. "It'd drive me bats in a week. I've got a flat of sorts in a low haunt behind Victoria—a poor thing, but mine own. But I keep an eye on Auntie V. I sometimes wonder if she'll be glad of a helping hand one day. It's a very odd set-up."

"I had a feeling it might be," said Jocelyn Truby.

II

I

"The old gentleman's in pretty good shape, Miss Delafield. Nothing to worry about at all."

Virgilia Delafield looked up from her desk as young Dr. Longaby crossed the studio. It was Longaby's first visit to Adrian Delafield, for Dr. Mareston (who had been paying a professional call weekly to examine the old painter) had recently had a severe stroke, and his young partner, Longaby, was doing all the jobs.

"Do sit down for a minute, Doctor," said Virgilia, in her deep abrupt voice. "I realise you're very busy—doctors always are—but I feel we should have a word together."

Longaby took the chair she indicated and glanced round the studio. Its walls were covered with gold-framed canvases, most of them very large: life-sized figures of romance—knights, pontiffs, ladies fair, nuns in flowing robes, goose girls in picturesque rags, looked ready to step from their canvases and perform a fancy dress measure in nightmarish fantasy.

"Never mind the pictures," said Miss Delafield. "I've got to the state when I don't even notice them, though you may find that hard to credit. Am I right in thinking that you are about to tell me that a weekly visit to my father is unnecessary?"

"Perfectly right," said Longaby promptly and cheerfully. He studied the grey-haired square-faced woman in front of him and decided that she looked a thoroughly sensible person.

"Your father is remarkably fit for his age," he went on. "I gather he had a slight seizure some years ago, but there's no indication of any further trouble along those lines, and I really don't think it's necessary for him to see a doctor unless his health deteriorates. He's not an invalid in any sense."

"I know," she said calmly. "It wasn't because of Father's health that I asked Dr. Mareston to call regularly every week. Didn't he discuss the case with you?"

"No. Mareston got a bit touchy as he aged: he regarded a few of his old patients as his own particular preserve, especially when they were notabilities, like your father. I did the surgeries and the most strenuous part of the practice and left Mareston to his own particular patients. It sometimes happens that way when an elderly doctor takes a young partner."

"Yes, yes. I follow," she said impatiently. "I shall have to explain—and trust you to respect my confidence. You saw Trimming, of course?"

"Why, yes. She's an unusual attendant: a trifle eccentric, I imagine, but very devoted, and she seems competent."

"Very competent: very devoted," said Miss Delafield tersely. "In place of a trifle eccentric I should say quite mad. When I asked Dr. Mareston to come to see my father regularly, it was because I thought some qualified person should keep an eye on Trimming."

Longaby did not answer immediately: he became aware that a situation which he had summed up as a bit odd might be more difficult than he had judged—but the elderly woman he was studying looked perfectly calm, not in the least a nervy or hysterical type.

"Did Mareston concur in your judgment?" he asked crisply.

"He did not think Trimming was mad," replied Miss Delafield calmly; "but he agreed with me it was desirable she should be supervised. He never saw her when she was unbalanced. Trimming is very shrewd."

"Well, having gone so far, I think you had better tell me exactly what you mean," said Longaby. "In what way is Trimming unbalanced?"

"She has religious mania, with all that that implies of excesses of exaltation and morbid depression, and she has what Dr. Mareston called 'a possessive complex.' She regards my father as her own possession. At one period she refused to let me see him, or to let anyone else see him. She carried this to such a degree that the neighbours and tradespeople believed he was dead. Some sensible person informed me of this rumour—and I interfered. It was after that that I arranged with Dr. Mareston for a weekly visit."

"I see," said Longaby, "and was Trimming—difficult?"

"Very difficult," said Virgilia. "I eventually fetched a policeman. He had no power to do anything of course, but the sight of a policeman's helmet made Trimming realise I meant business."

Longaby laughed: he couldn't help it. Miss Virgilia Delafield, sixty-ish, bespectacled, don-ish in voice and appearance, seemed so remote from police constables and religious mania alike.

"Dr. Mareston dealt with Trimming very competently," went on Virgilia. "She used to spend hours praying at my father's bedside, to say nothing of weeping over his prospects in her postulated hereafter. Really, I often marvelled that his own mind was not affected."

"Why didn't he sack her?" asked Longaby.

"Because he has depended on her for thirty-five years," went on Virgilia. "She has coddled and cosseted him, cooked his food and cleaned his house, washed his shirts and cut his hair. He says he can't do without her." She broke off and studied Longaby in her detached analytical way. "Don't imagine I'm asking your co-operation to get rid of Trimming," she went on. "Quite the contrary. It would be nothing short of cruelty to deprive my father of her services; and sentiment apart, where should I be likely to find another woman who would run the house, do the cooking, nurse, tend and dress a very old man who is often very unpleasant in his habits?"

"You wouldn't," said Longaby. "But just where do I come in?"

"You supply the necessary supervision," said Virgilia primly. "Let me make myself clear. A woman like Trimming, despite her addiction to puritan virtues and her convictions about absolute chastity, takes much more notice of a man than a woman when it comes to the voice of authority. If I remonstrate with Trimming she responds with abuse. She 'creates,' as my young nephew says. A curious idiom... But when Dr. Mareston said, 'It won't do, Trimming. If this goes on we shall have to make other arrangements,' she believed him. She believed he had the power to implement his remarks; and she knew quite well that Dr. Mareston observed her pretty closely."

Again Longaby chuckled: he was enjoying Miss Delafield's own "curious idiom." "I see your point," he said; "but you'd better tell me where Trimming is to toe the line. Does she pinch the spoons, to put it vulgarly?"

"Dear me, no," said Virgilia, "and if she did I shouldn't worry. It's her behaviour. When the fit takes her she indulges in prolonged weepings; also aggressive abstinence—she fasts for a week at a time and her work suffers in consequence. I have seen her staggering round the house as though she were inebriated."

"Was she?" put in Dr. Longaby. "I've known it happen, you know."

"I have no evidence to that effect," said Virgilia, "and Dr. Mareston was satisfied that such was not the case, but after her prolonged fasts she has fits of morbid melancholy. It is on these occasions that I feel most apprehensive."

"Why? Do you think she is capable of violence—to your father, for instance?"

"She would never hurt my father. I am convinced of that," replied Virgilia. "She is devoted to him. She might try to murder me, of course. She could easily convince herself that she was doing the Lord's work in eliminating me. But I do not anticipate anything of that nature. She might, however, commit suicide. Melancholics are prone to do so; and it would be excessively unpleasant."

"Excessively," said Longaby dryly. "Has she ever had a shot at it?"

Watching Virgilia Delafield closely, Longaby had a shrewd guess that he was getting to the crux of this particular problem.

"I should scruple to state that she has actually attempted to take her own life," said Virgilia carefully; "but there was an occasion when Dr. Mareston was much concerned. He had been giving her sedative tablets of some kind after a bout of religious exhibitionism. I was not in residence here at the time, but he did tell me that he had discontinued the treatment and given Trimming a good talking to."

"If she'd really tried to put herself out, he'd have told you," said Longaby. "Perhaps she practised a bit of exhibitionism with the tablets. Incidentally, has the woman always been peculiar? If she's been with your father for thirty-five years you've had plenty of time to observe her."

"But I have not lived in this household over that period," said Virgilia. "I am now sixty-three. I have not lived with my father since I went to Cambridge at the age of nineteen—in 1911 that was. He was very unwilling for me to follow an academic career, and to put it shortly there was a family row and I was cast out with contumely. I have seen my father at intervals since 1920, when Trimming came here, but there was a long period—nearly twenty years—when I was overseas, and I did not see him at all. It is only in the last few years that I have considered it my duty to see how things went with him, and just nine months since I moved into this studio."

"How did your father take it when you came here?"

"I think he was glad," she replied. "I could not have come here to live without his consent, of course, and it was all a great nuisance to me, but I did realise that he was terrified of Trimming. After all, he *is* my father, and women of my generation were brought up with a sense of duty." She broke off and then added more tersely: "But I do not wish to burden you with my personal history. All that I ask is that you should call here at fairly frequent intervals and see my father."

"And keep an eye on Trimming," he said. "If I'm to do that, Miss Delafield, I shall need to get to know her. Do you object to my talking to her, so that I can form my own opinion?"

"Indeed, no!" she exclaimed. "That is what I want you to do. It will be very tiresome. You will have to listen to a spate of abuse directed against me. I am, incidentally, an agnostic, and I have lived my life according to my own code of conduct—not Trimming's. 'Spawn of Satan' is one of her milder epithets for me."

"I shall give her every encouragement to say anything she likes to say," said Longaby. "The more outspokenly abusive she is, the better: it will put me in a good position to deal with her." He glanced at Virgilia Delafield's strong calm face and added: "I am afraid this must be all very unpalatable for you, to put it mildly. I respect your sense of duty. Most women of your age would have left things alone and hoped for the best."

"Thank you, but I don't want you to think of me as a martyr to duty," replied Virgilia tartly. "I have no objection to this studio as living accommodation—except for the pictures, of course. But, as I told you, I have got to the state of ignoring them. I am quite independent of the house. I have adequate cooking and washing facilities in the old model's room, and the place is very quiet. As a writer, I value quietude."

"I'm sure you do," said Longaby. "So you don't come across Trimming over the ordinary domestic routine, then?"

"In no way. I have scrupulously avoided interfering with her arrangements. She is, I admit freely, an excellent manager and a first-class cook, save when her mania possesses her. But I go in to see my father every day, and I chose my own times for visiting him. This means that I can observe Trimming if she behaves unreasonably. If you will co-operate to the extent of one weekly call—*not* on the same day or at the same hour each week, I think we can carry on quite satisfactorily."

"I'll do my best," said Longaby. "Actually, I shall be interested to observe Trimming. Is it Miss Trimming?"

"It certainly is," said Virgilia. She got up and stood beside him, a square, sturdy figure, upright, well balanced on her feet, neat and businesslike in a well-cut dark suit, with her grey hair cropped short and brushed back hard from a broad forehead.

"Trimming resented it bitterly when I took possession of this studio," she went on. "She had rigged it up as a sort of oratory or place of devotion and I gather she had meetings of her particular cult here. I have never discovered the exact nature of her denomination—something at once esoteric and primitive, I believe. But she will doubtless tell you about her sense of outrage at my presence here."

"Wouldn't it be pleasanter for you without the pictures?" asked Longaby.

Virgilia laughed. "It certainly would, Dr. Longaby, but had I moved the pictures, had I even touched them, I think Trimming would have taken direct action—possibly with her meat chopper. She has a very adequate chopper. I'm not exaggerating," she added calmly. "The woman is mad; but while her madness permits her to carry out her duties and care for my father, I am prepared to disregard it."

"I don't feel very happy about it," said Longaby. "If you are right, and the woman is really deranged, you might be faced with very real trouble. Have you a telephone in the studio?"

"A telephone? Dear me, no. There is not one in the house, either. But I beg that you will not concern yourself over me, Doctor—that was not my intention at all. I am quite capable of looking after myself. In any case, once the door is locked, the studio is quite self-contained, and I never go over to the house after dark."

"It must be rather depressing for you," said Longaby. "Have you no relative who could take some of the burden off your shoulders?"

"My only relative, to the best of my knowledge and belief, is my nephew, Roy Braithwaite. I have no doubt he would help in an emergency, but if you are suggesting that I should have someone to live here with me, I can only tell you that there is nothing I should dislike more. I am a natural solitary and I cherish my solitude."

"Well, everybody has to decide their own manner of life," rejoined Longaby. "Meanwhile, I am glad you have confided in me, and I will make it my business to come and see Miss Trimming shortly. I will, of course, report to you if I consider any action should be taken."

"Thank you, Doctor. As to any action—the only action which seems likely to simplify the present situation is the removal of one of the three of us—in a box, as they say. Though whether it will be my father or myself or Trimming who heads the procession is an open question and one which I decline to bother about."

2

"Mad? My dear chap, she's as mad as a hatter. Has been for years. Mareston knew all about it. He and I were old cronies, you know. He told me a lot of things he would never have told anyone else."

Admiral Bevenham was another of Dr. Mareston's private patients ("old chronics" Longaby called them). The admiral was eighty-three and had been bedridden with arthritis for some years, but his mind was lively enough. Longaby had had no difficulty in getting the admiral to talk about the ménage at Firenze, and now the old sailor was well set.

"She sees things," he went on; "apparitions and spirits, you know, and she holds long conversations with them. On one occasion she moved a lot of furniture out into the garden and built up a sort of pulpit with a circle of chairs all round it. She then mounted the pulpit and addressed the non-existent congregation and called each one by name and mentioned their individual sins. The postman heard her at it—he said it gave him the willies. Raving mad, she was."

"There's madness and madness," said Longaby. "In spite of all her peculiarities, she seems to run the house very competently and to look after the old man exceedingly well. He's tending to senility, but she keeps him clean and wholesome and he's obviously well fed and in good condition."

"Of course he is!" said the admiral. "Trimming slaves for him. You know, I think it'd have been better if the daughter hadn't butted in. She's simply an irritant, and, anyway, Trimming's been looking after the old chap for donkey's years—to say nothing of what she did in getting him home when the Huns overran France."

"I didn't hear about that," said Longaby.

"Must have been an epic," said the admiral. "Delafield had been living in France for some time: his London house was shut up and he'd got a villa at Passy—I think it was Passy. Anyway, she got him to the coast somehow. Mareston swore she loaded him into a wheelbarrow before they got through, kitted up as an old peasant. He'd had a seizure or something and his legs went. Quite a story! Of course she'd got the needful—he made a pot of money in his time."

"So I gathered—though she's careful enough now, judging from the way the house is run. Anything in that?" mused Longaby. "Is Trimming expecting to scoop the lot?"

The admiral chuckled. "Don't you believe it! The old chap realised all his capital and bought an annuity—he told Mareston so. 'Encourage 'em to keep me alive if they know there's nothing to follow,' he said—his very words. And Miss Virgilia knows it. She's not there for what she can get. Neither's Trimming—though I believe he's left his canvases to Trimming, God help her!"

"It's quite a story," said Longaby, "though I have an uncomfortable feeling it's a situation which may develop in a very unpleasant way. After all, this Trimming isn't normal."

"No. She's mad," said the admiral cheerfully, "but so are lots of us. Anyway, her sort of madness keeps old Delafield pretty cosy, I believe, and if Trimming likes to preach to the furniture, no one's any the worse. As for the daughter, she's a proper blue-stocking, I hear: far too learned to give the old man his blanket baths and all the rest of the doings."

"What's her subject?" asked Longaby.

"Medieval history. She's been a university lecturer most of her life, and written books which only scholars can read. She's an atheist, I'm told, but her speciality is the rise of Protestantism— the convictions which made Wycliffe and the Lollards get cracking—theological stuff. It's a funny world, Doc, but don't tell me an academic dame who gets all worked up over that sort of stuff's going to be any comfort to an aged reprobate whose internal workings are his major preoccupation. Better have left it to Trimming."

Again Dr. Longaby laughed, and the admiral joined in.

"Poor old codger!" he said. "I'm not a profane man, but when I think of Trimming praying over him and wrestling for his soul— and for all I know his soul may need a bit of wrestling for—and his daughter de-praying, if I may put it that way—well, it makes me count my blessings."

"Don't be too hard on the daughter," said Longaby. "So far as I can gather, she is impelled by a sense of duty to live in circumstances which would drive most elderly women frantic—and she's keeping admirably calm and making the best of it."

"But she needn't have gone there," said the admiral. "Elderly women with a sense of duty are the devil," he added.

"I don't know," said Longaby. "Once she knew that her father was at the mercy of a woman who is certainly a maniac in some respects, it wasn't easy for her to disregard the situation. However, we'll see if we can keep things going. Miss Delafield seems convinced that Trimming is amenable to the voice of the authority—male authority, that is."

"They're all the same that way," chuckled the admiral.

III

I

"BUT I'M DELIGHTED TO SEE YOU, MR. TRUBY," SAID Virgilia Delafield. "There are so few people who remember my father, and fewer still who take the trouble to come to inquire after him." She glanced round the studio and made a gesture towards the pictures on the wall. "Of course, I know that these things are a matter for mirth to the younger generation, and as objects to live with they are quite dreadful in their exuberant realism, but my father did earn the admiration of his contemporaries—and I find it sad that he is forgotten."

"But he's not forgotten," said Jocelyn Truby firmly. "I, for instance, still hold him in regard. Admittedly these pictures, hung in such close juxtaposition, have an element of hyperbole—if I may put it that way. But considered separately, what mastery, what draughtsmanship!"

"The Academicians of my father's period could certainly draw," she admitted smilingly. "I often wonder if it was that which caused their eclipse—excess of virtuosity. Now would you really like to see my father, Mr. Truby? I have to warn you that he is sadly changed."

"We've all changed," said Jocelyn cheerfully. "If your father remembers me at all—and I know it's most unlikely—he would envisage me as a rubicund young lieutenant in outmoded military uniform with a lot of brass buttons. In fact, of the two of us, I must have changed much more than he has in the past thirty-five years."

"How kind you are!" said Virgilia Delafield. "I sometimes think that kindness is a virtue which is as outmoded as drawing."

"Bless you, nothing of the kind!" he replied. "That niece of mine—Susan—she's the kindest soul I know."

"She's a very beautiful young woman," said Virgilia. "It's a long time since I've seen anybody whose face has given me so much pleasure, and I am delighted to know that my nephew can value such beauty when he sees it. Shall we leave them to wander in the 'cypress walk,' as that charming child puts it? It pleases me so much that any young person has absorbed Tennyson into her speech."

"Let us leave them by all means," said Jocelyn. "There is something about your nephew which I enjoy. He's a courteous lad."

"Yes. He has retained something of his mother's gentleness," replied Virgilia. "She was my sister of course: a very charming personality, and it was sad for her that her husband died when Roy was so young, but she brought up her two boys very sensibly."

"Who was the father?" asked Jocelyn.

"Michael Braithwaite was in the Consular service," she replied. "He was very able, but unfortunately his health was permanently undermined in the First World War, and he was an invalid for some years before he died. Mifanwy really kept the family going. She wrote romantic novels under the name of Rosamund Casterton."

"Good gracious! I remember the name," said Jocelyn. "My sister Di loved her books, but I had no idea the author was Adrian Delafield's daughter."

"She was very careful to conceal the fact," said Virgilia dryly. "Her novels were pure pot boilers—quite devoid of literary merit—but she kept her sick husband and educated her boys from the proceeds. Now, shall we go across to the house? I think this is the one time of year when the garden still looks charming—the daffodils come up year after year."

She opened a door which led into the garden and Jocelyn Truby gave an exclamation of pleasure: the covered way which led from the studio to the house was like a timbered cloister: the timbering of the roof was dark and heavy and great upright baulks supported it, in place of the clustered pillars of a stone-built cloister walk. Each of the lights had a wrought ironwork grille, and vine leaves were already spreading their fine-cut greenery against the elaboration of the ironwork.

"But this is beautiful," exclaimed Jocelyn.

"I find it charming, in its dated Gothic manner," rejoined Virgilia. "There is a door half-way along. You might like to see the roofing tiles: my father brought them back from Italy—real Roman pantiles. The ironwork is Italian, too, and that well-head—though, of course, there is no well."

They went into the garden through a wrought-iron gate and Jocelyn stood back to look at the tiled roof—its original terra-cotta hue now blackened by half a century of London soot. Behind him, rough unmown grass stretched to the decrepit cypress walk, and in the centre of the plot a Florentine well-head and containing wall added a touch of fantasy, with daffodils shining round the Roman bonding of the brickwork. Susan and Roy were sitting on the low circular wall in the sunshine, looking at the decrepit cypresses.

"I know it's one of those artificial contrivances characteristic of a pseudo-romantic period," said Virgilia; "but it is still pleasing to the eye."

"It is, indeed," said Jocelyn. "Pre-functional, pre-ferro-concrete, pre-steel girder, pre the dehumanised school. I admit without shame that it delights me."

"It's a pity the garden has gone to ruin," said Virgilia. "Trimming cares nothing about gardens, except as an area of interment for her sequence of cats. How I hate cats—quite unreasonably, of course. It's a constitutional peculiarity. I always ring the bell when I come to the house—just as a measure of courtesy. I have a key, and Trimming knows it, but I try to keep our relations on a mannerly plane. You remember Trimming?"

"I do, indeed."

"Good. She will like to see an old friend."

Virgilia Delafield stood outside an iron-studded door set in a Gothic archway and pulled a wrought-iron bell handle. From within came a deep jangle, a surprisingly loud note from a bell which was obviously cracked.

"Cracked," said Virgilia in her abrupt deep voice. "Pure Alice in Wonderland, all of it, including ourselves. I am mad, you are mad, we are all mad. I don't wish to talk in terms of hyperbole, to use your excellent word, but I never hear that bell without the word 'cracked' coming into my mind, and in my youth cracked was a synonym for the 'bats' and 'crackers,' the 'loopy' and 'haywire' of to-day. I often think our idiom was more concise and expressive… Ah, here is Trimming."

There was a squeak and a grind, and then a small Judas panel, set behind an iron grille, was shot back, and Jocelyn Truby caught a glimpse of a white face and dark deep-set eyes before the heavy door was opened with a groaning of hinges almost hyperbolical in itself.

"Good afternoon, Trimming," said Virgilia. "Mr. Truby is an old friend of my father's, and would like to see him, if Father is well enough to receive him."

Trimming stood in the Gothic doorway, and it flashed across Jocelyn Truby's mind that she looked like a black and white illustration in a novel of early Victorian vintage. Not a medieval figure, but a Victorian draughtsman's conception of medievalism, even to the thin scrawny lines beloved of that period. She was a tall woman, exaggeratedly thin, as though composed of fretwork boards superimposed to give the substance of solidity. From chin to feet she was clothed in rusty black, relieved only by a white tucker at the neck and a "chatelaine" of dull silver hung with keys and scissors and other oddments hanging from her waist. Her face was thin and pallid, her eyes jet black, deep-set under heavy brows, and she wore a black silk veil round her forehead and drawn severely behind her ears, the veil also edged with a white tucker. Jocelyn had braced himself to face something bizarre and he had himself well in hand.

"Good afternoon, Trimming. You won't remember me, though I remember you. I saw you in 1920 when Mr. Delafield invited me to his studio to see a picture he had painted, commissioned by my old regiment. I am very happy to see you again."

Trimming bobbed—a deliberate old-fashioned bob, suitable to pay respect to a lord spiritual. With downcast eyes she whispered:

"It is a privilege to see the master's old friends, sir. The painting was called 'The Glorious Tenth.' The sketch the master made for it is still in the library. Will you trouble to step inside, sir." Truby stood to one side and Virgilia preceded him, passing Trimming so close that tweed skirt brushed rusty black frock.

"Take Mr. Truby up to my father, Trimming. I won't go in with him, but I should like to see the repairs the plasterer has been doing to the ceiling in the drawing-room." She spoke perfectly normally, but Trimming gave no sign that she had heard. Virgilia turned to Truby. "If you will go on up, I want to look at the repairs. These old houses suffer from dampness. You will find me down here after you have seen Father. He can't talk for more than a few minutes."

"Please to come upstairs, sir," said Trimming.

Her voice was very odd, deep and husky, but reduced to a breathy whisper. As Truby followed her upstairs, walking on a well-kept drugget which covered a Turkey carpet, Truby said:

"I'd like a word with you before I see Mr. Delafield, Trimming. It's hardly likely that he will remember me."

"Indeed, sir, he does remember you. Miss Delafield mentioned you might be calling. It was the picture brought it back, sir. He never forgets one of his pictures. I took the sketch—the cartoon he calls it—up to him, and he pointed you out. I understand all the officers in the picture were portraits."

"Excellent!" said Truby. "How is he, Trimming? He's a great age and I expect he has his bad days."

They paused on the landing, and Trimming said: "In himself, he's wonderfully well, sir. I look after him: indeed, I do. I guard him. I know I have to, for there are powers of evil in this house. While I'm here, no evil shall come nigh him."

Jocelyn was aware of a sense of discomfort incommensurate with the occasion: after all, he knew that Trimming was a bit mad—Roy had made that plain enough—and her allusions to powers of evil was the commonplace of her type of mind, but he suddenly shivered and felt that the house was unreasonably cold. He had noticed it as he came in, out of the sunshine into the shadowed hall with the tiled floor. Here, on the landing, the chill of the hall seemed to rise like an emanation—and it was no use telling himself that cold air does not rise.

"You feel it, sir," whispered the husky voice beside him. "It's not an earthly chill; it's the cold of the darkness that knows not light."

"I hope you keep Mr. Delafield's room warm," said Jocelyn with asperity. "As one ages, one feels the cold, and neither you nor I is as young as we used to be, Trimming. Now take me in to your master."

She moved forward silently, her black list slippers making no sound, her rusty black frock no rustle. "Damn the woman! She's enough to give anybody the blue willies," said Jocelyn to himself, using an "idiom" of Susan's to cheer himself up. The handle of a door was turned without sound and a waft of warm air came out of the shadows beyond the door—a warmth with a medicated antiseptic smell which Joseph disliked exceedingly.

"It's Mr. Truby, sir," whispered Trimming hoarsely.

"Come in, come in," said a gruff and quavery voice. "Pull that curtain back a little, Trimming. He'll think you've got me laid out before my time."

It was a big room, but the curtains were drawn so as to exclude most of the daylight, and it was as uncomfortably warm as the entrance and landing had been uncomfortably cold. Much of the floor space was taken up by an immense four-poster bed, whose heavy hangings still further obstructed the light, and Jocelyn Truby had his work cut out to reach the corner whence the old man's voice had sounded. He sat in a big winged "grandfather" chair, with rugs piled over his knees, and at first all that Jocelyn could recognise of the old painter was his pointed white beard and his wrinkled white hands, for despite the gloom of the room, Adrian Delafield wore an eyeshade round his forehead.

"Young Truby?" he quavered. "I remember you perfectly. You got the M.C. for oustandingly gallant conduct on Vimy Ridge. Sit down, sit down. Trimming, go and fetch that cartoon. Glad to see you. Very good of you to come." A wrinkled tremulous hand was held out and Jocelyn clasped it gingerly and found it unpleasantly soft and warm.

"Trimming, do as you're told. Get that cartoon for the captain and don't stand gibbering there," went on Delafield. Trimming glided soundlessly out and the quavering voice went on:

"Devil take her! If I didn't take care she'd stand over me all day long, wrestling in prayer. But she can cook. I tell you she can cook. Can't stand slops, never could, young Truby. Venables, he was your colonel, and Smith-Blackson was adjutant. Then Major Weldon was at the firing-step—that right?"

"Perfectly correct," agreed Jocelyn Truby. "You have a wonderful memory, sir."

"Never forget anybody who sat to me for a portrait," said Delafield. "Go and stand by the window, Truby. Pull those damned curtains back a little—not too far. My eyes give me a lot of trouble. Yes. I can see now. I suppose you *are* Truby? You've altered."

"It's over thirty-five years ago," said Jocelyn Truby. "I was twenty-five then; now I'm over sixty. Good gracious! What was that?"

A heavy thud had shaken the whole room, followed by a clatter, and Truby exclaimed: "Trimming must have fallen downstairs."

"Not she. Trimming never falls down anything," rejoined Delafield callously. "You might think she would but she doesn't. It's those decorators. They're always dropping something. What was that noise, Trimming?"

Before Truby was aware of it, Trimming was back in the room, clasping a framed picture in her arms. "It's the plasterer, sir. He has trouble with the ladders. There was no need to have it done…"

"That'll do. That'll do. Don't whine. Put the cartoon where the captain can see it."

Trimming held the picture by the window and Truby went and looked at the first sketch for "The Glorious Tenth." It looked singularly unreal, this Academician's sketch of "Going over the top" in the trench warfare of 1916. But there was the drawing of himself, and Venables and Smith-Blackson, all looking incredibly young. "I expect the War Museum has put the painting down in the cellars," thought Truby. "I must say it looks an odd relic if it's anything like this. And was I once like that?"

He was about to speak to the old painter, trying to form a phrase of appreciation about the preposterous picture which Trimming held as though it were a religious relic, when a long-drawn sound made him realise that amiable amenities would be wasted; Adrian Delafield was snoring: he had slipped into the easy sleep of advanced age.

"He's like that, sir," said Trimming. "Wide awake one moment and fast asleep the next. It's the Lord's will," she added.

"Quite; quite. Better not disturb him," said Jocelyn, whose one wish was to get outside the warm, medicated stuffiness and funereal gloom of the bedroom. "What shall I do with this?"

He indicated the cartoon of "The Glorious Tenth," to which he had taken an unreasoning dislike.

"I will see to it, sir. If you will excuse me, I'll stay here with the master. I don't like leaving him. I always think he might slip away, and there's evil lurking here…"

"Of course, of course. Miss Delafield will be waiting for me downstairs…"

"Yes, she'll be waiting, the Lord keep you," said Trimming.

2

When Jocelyn Truby reached the stairhead, he saw with consternation that Virgilia Delafield was sitting on the bottom stairs, her grey head bent in her hands. She got up as he came downstairs and stood by the newel post, and Jocelyn saw that her coat was marked with plaster and then that there was a contusion on her forehead.

"I'm so sorry," she said. "I must have shifted one of the ladders in there, and a board fell down and struck me. All very tiresome, but it might have been worse. Let us get out into the sunshine again. This house always feels like a vault."

Jocelyn was full of concern. He didn't like the story of a ladder which shifted at all, and he did not think the well-balanced and composed Virgilia was the sort of woman to blunder into a ladder. When they got outside into the covered way he said:

"I am indeed distressed that you should have suffered such a misfortune. Is there anything I can do to assist?"

"Please don't worry: it was just one of those foolish things which seem to happen in this house," she replied, and then added with energy, "and for goodness' sake don't suggest that it wasn't an accident. The only way I can go on living here is to assume that things are normal until I have any proof that they are abnormal. Let us go and sit by the well for a moment."

They crossed the rough grass and Jocelyn Truby was conscious of a sense of relief when he heard Susan's voice and Roy's laughter somewhere behind the "moth-eaten cypresses." The cold house and the hot bedroom had made a strong impression on Jocelyn, and it wasn't a comfortable impression.

"I always think that certain things happen to certain people," said Miss Delafield, as she seated herself on the low wall around the "well." "Trimming, an excellent cook and housekeeper, is a complete maniac in some respects. The consequence is that whenever a workman is sent here, whether plumber or builder or painter, you can be quite sure of one thing—the workman will be a moron. They always are. Trimming attracts halfwits as fruit attracts wasps."

"Dear me," said Jocelyn unhappily.

"I've observed it several times," went on Virgilia calmly. "This man who is doing the plastering is quite a good workman, but if he's not a mental defective, then I've never seen one. Of course, he left his gear badly placed and the floorboards in that room are loose. I stood on a wobbly floorboard and the ladder shifted. I fear my only regret is that it wasn't Trimming who got the subsequent bump."

"But are you quite sure it wasn't Trimming who shifted the ladder?" asked Jocelyn.

"Quite sure," replied Virgilia firmly. "She didn't come into the room at all."

Before Jocelyn had time to reply, Susan and Roy appeared from behind a bank of overgrown shrubs and Susan came forward to speak to Virgilia.

"I think the garden's entrancing, Miss Delafield. It's marvellously 'period.' It reminds me of some Rosetti drawings my mother used to show me when I was small, all overgrown arbours and distressed damosels or sleeping beauties in a tangle of thickets."

Virgilia Delafield laughed. "That's a very acute observation, my dear. I remember those pen drawings and this garden has just the Rosetti quality—a rather messy fantasy. But it surprises me that you are so well acquainted with the painters and poets of the last century. Most young things of your age are unaware that Dante Gabriel Rosetti ever existed—and Tennyson is anathema to them."

"Oh, but I had Uncle Jocelyn to tell me stories and show me pictures," she rejoined, "and I think I'm old-fashioned by nature. I get so tired of all the contemporary clevers."

"Anyway, Rosetti and Tennyson are having a comeback," said Roy; "but talking about fantasies, was that huroosh we heard inside there a fantasy? I thought the house was falling down."

"Don't exaggerate," said Virgilia coldly. "One of the decorator's ladders fell down."

"On you?" demanded Roy, eyeing the plaster on his aunt's coat. "You mean that the Neanderthal of a plasterer dropped things on you? I think that's a bit too much—and I bet Trimming put him up to it."

"Don't talk nonsense!" exclaimed Virgilia. "Nobody was in the room when it happened: it was my own clumsiness."

"Sez you," said Roy sceptically. "I shall have a word with Trimming about this. She's far more afraid of me than she is of you."

"Really, Roy, you might consider the effect your conversation is having on our guests," said Virgilia severely. "They will think this is a madhouse."

"Well, isn't it? Meaning the house," rejoined Roy. "Nobody who has ever set eyes on Trimming is left with any room for doubt." He turned back to Susan. "Sorry; I'm always being told not to exaggerate. Would you really like to look at the pictures in the studio? You haven't got to, you know."

"That's what I came for," said Susan deflatingly. She smiled at Virgilia. "Please, do you mind, Miss Delafield. It's your studio, not Roy's. May I go and look at the pictures?"

"Bless you, of course you may, my dear," rejoined Virgilia. "Go along and chuckle. I still chuckle myself sometimes."

Susan and Roy went off over the unkempt grass, but Jocelyn put a hand on Virgilia's arm.

"I don't want to bother you, Miss Delafield, but I can't help feeling troubled. Trimming made a very disagreeable impression on me."

"Of course she did. All normal people feel discomfort in the presence of the abnormal," replied Virgilia. "Trimming is a horror—but she's a very competent manager. I only hope that I shall be able to prevent my nephew from interfering. He has a most unfortunate effect on her."

"Is she afraid of him?" asked Jocelyn hopefully.

"Not in the least. My own belief is that she dotes on him. If Roy speaks sharply to her, Trimming wilts—though she doesn't alter her ways. But if he goes too far—and the young have no sense of proportion—Trimming will go melancholy and subside into penance and fasting. My own belief is that she is a flagellant."

"Good gracious!" exclaimed Jocelyn Truby.

"I can put up with Trimming on most occasions, but Trimming bewailing her sins is more than I can stomach," said Virgilia. "Besides, it ruins her cooking and demoralises her work. So it's easier if we all keep very calm and avoid both recriminations and protestations. Why, what an astounding noise! Surely that can't be Trimming practising a last trump…"

"I think it's only a motor horn, a klaxon as they now call them. Presumably it is that young friend of Susan's who was to call for her in his car."

"Oh! I see," rejoined Virgilia calmly. "Perhaps Roy primed him with some of his more outrageous exaggerations and the noise we hear is in the nature of a rescue attempt."

"I can only say that it is outrageously unmannerly," said Jocelyn indignantly. To his great relief, Virgilia Delafield laughed aloud.

"Do you know, I find it rather refreshing," she said, dabbing at eyes that were moist with laughter. "I know I'm slightly ridiculous myself; a pedantic elderly spinster living in a studio adorned with the canvases of a bygone period. The house is ridiculous, so is my father. And Trimming is pure farce. But I doubt if any of it is quite so ridiculous as the young man who is making all that noise because he believes you are incapable of safeguarding your niece in the home of a Victorian painter."

"I think that is very well put," said Jocelyn. "It cheers me up too. I know the young *do* find us ridiculous, but how pleasant it is to be able to observe that they also can be ludicrous."

Nevertheless, as Jocelyn walked away under the budding lime trees of St. John's Wood (having firmly refused a lift in Peter Raven's preposterously large car, and having said a few terse words on the subject of redundant noise), he did rather wonder if Trimming were really "pure farce." If so, he had a feeling that it was the sort of farce he did not enjoy.

IV

I

"I'M SORRY TO INTERRUPT YOU, MISS DELAFIELD, BUT I'VE rung and knocked at the front door of the house, and I can't get any answer," said Dr. Longaby. "Perhaps Trimming is out—I'm a bit earlier than usual."

Virgilia Delafield looked surprised. "That's very unusual," she said. "Trimming always goes out very early, as soon as the shops are open. I'll take you in by the covered way. I insisted on having a key—just in case. Of course, if Trimming is busy with my father she would disregard the bell. I have often waited an unconscionable time for her to open the door."

"How have things been going?" asked Dr. Longaby.

"Oh, quite reasonably. I think Trimming has a real respect for you, Doctor; but she has been showing signs of a penitential mood, so I'm glad to see you. Trimming in sackcloth is a real trial."

They walked along the covered way to the iron-studded door, and Miss Delafield seized the bell handle and tugged it vigorously, so that they heard the bell inside jangling like a mad thing.

"It's a dreadful sound, isn't it?" said Virgilia. "A sort of clang of doom. But my father is immensely proud of the bell. He got it in Sicily."

"It's a most interesting house, full of unusual things," said Longaby, and Virgilia replied:

"Junk, pure junk. The collection of one generation is the junk of the next: it takes a century or two before junk acquires the status of the genuine antique. Really, I think Trimming is keeping us waiting on purpose," she added irritably. "I shall ring once more and then open the door."

The cracked bell clanged again and Longaby thought to himself: "I wondered if this would happen one of these days... And if Trimming's bunged herself and the old man full of barbiturates I shall get a raspberry from the coroner."

Virgilia had produced her big key and the doctor heard the wards shoot back noisily, but the door did not open; she shook it vigorously, and then said:

"Really, the woman is maddening; the door is bolted on the inside—I told her she was never to bolt it."

"The thing is, we've got to get inside the house somehow," said Longaby quietly, after shaking the door in his turn. "There may have been an accident."

"Yes," agreed Virgilia, still quite calmly. "That wretched man has finished in the drawing-room, doing the plastering. Perhaps the shutters are unfastened—all the other ground-floor windows are barred."

She led the way, through the wrought-iron gate in the covered way, across the grass and around the angle of the house to the south front where the windows gave on to a tiled terrace. Longaby saw at once that the shutters were closed inside the glass doors of the French window and for the first time Virgilia Delafield showed signs of unease.

"It does look as though something's wrong," she said.

"It does," agreed Longaby. "I shall have to break in. I can kick the glass in, but the shutters may be more difficult. I'll go and get a spanner or tyre lever from my car... You said you hadn't a telephone, didn't you?"

Without waiting for an answer, he ran across the garden to the studio, which had its own entrance from the road. He had driven his car round to this entrance and, as he gained the pavement, he looked up and down the sunny peaceful road, hoping to see a policeman, or a milkman—or anyone who could help. But there was no one in sight, and he knew the house beyond Firenze was empty and derelict, waiting for the housebreakers.

"Damn!" he thought. "Whatever I do will probably be wrong, but I'm going to break in. I shall probably find the house is full of gas..."

He raced back, having snatched the tools which seemed most likely to be useful, and found Virgilia waiting on the terrace.

"All the windows are shut and the milk hasn't been taken in," she said. "Trimming generally gets up at crack o' dawn..."

Longaby kicked the glass in; it was good plate glass and took a lot of smashing, and it made a lot of noise. "Surely somebody will hear the din," he thought, as he knocked out dangerous jags of glass with the heavy spanner. Then he got his tyre lever between the shutters and wrestled with it until the stubborn wood cracked. It seemed to take an age before, with a crack like a pistol shot, the fastening gave and the shutters swung back suddenly, so that he was almost precipitated into the room. His first reaction was "No gas... Thank the Lord for small mercies." Longaby had once been the first to enter a house where two women had killed themselves by turning on the gas taps, and it wasn't an experience he wanted to repeat. His next thought was, "What the hell's been happening here?"

The room seemed to be draped in whiteness—floor, furniture, everything. Then Longaby remembered the plasterer, and realised the furniture and chandelier were draped in dust sheets, and the rest of the room in dust. He heard Virgilia Delafield's voice.

"Dear me... the cornice has fallen." And Longaby saw that large chunks of white plaster were lying on the floor, but he hurried across the big room and dragged the door open against the pile of plaster debris and looked across the gloomy hall.

Trimming was lying prone on the floor at the foot of the stairs; she looked very long and very black, and Longaby knew that she was dead before he touched her, for her head was twisted on her neck in a manner which told its own tale. Just clear of her head a tray lay on the floor and broken crockery and glass strewed the tiles. There was the remains of a white stream of milk or soup which had trickled across the tiles and Longaby saw with repugnance that a big black cat was just slinking away after licking up the congealed liquid. He heard Virgilia catch her breath behind him as he knelt beside the body to examine it.

"Poor soul... Is she badly hurt?" she asked.

"She's dead; she's been dead for hours," said Longaby, as he touched one rigid outflung arm.

Virgilia gave a cry. "For hours? What about Father?"

In a trice, she was rushing upstairs and the doctor heard her laboured breath as she pounded up, heavily, as the middle-aged do.

"Here, steady. Don't kill yourself too," he cried.

As he ran up behind her, he caught her just as she tripped over a brass stair rail, where the drugget was ruckled up, but she recovered and turned at the stair head towards the second short flight which led to the landing window and Adrian Delafield's bedroom door. The old painter was lying on the stairs, head downwards, feet on the landing, as though he had collapsed in the effort to get downstairs.

"He heard her fall and tried to reach her... Poor old Father," she gasped.

Longaby's hands touched the white head. "He's not dead. But

if he's been lying like that for long, he'll be in a bad way," he said, seeing the contused face. "Can you help me lift him?"

"Of course. Tell me what to do."

He heard Virgilia's laboured breathing and glanced at her face, and then said: "If we could get him flat, on the landing floor, that would be best. Then I will go for help."

It was a grim struggle getting the old man lifted; he was surprisingly heavy, and Virgilia was very little help, for all her efforts. Longaby dared not lift the sagging body over his shoulder—the doctor guessed that it would take very little to extinguish the faint flame of life which still, surprisingly, flickered in the helpless body. As he toiled, slowly and patiently, Longaby thought: "The woman must have fallen last night; she's been dead for twelve hours at least... But there's no light on. Did she carry things up and down those stairs in the dark?"

He knew there was no electric light in the house—only gas, and the fitments were about fifty years old. Then, when he had a chance of raising his head, he saw that there was a fish-tail flame burning in one of the preposterous flambeau-like fitments on the landing, almost imperceptible in the daylight which shone from the landing window.

At last they got the old man flat on his back and Longaby said: "Get some blankets from his bed—and hot-water bottles if you can find them. I'll go and get my case and give him an injection—his pulse is very faint... Wait a minute, I'll pull back the curtains in the bedroom, it's dark in there."

There was a gas jet burning in the bedroom, too, under a green shade. Longaby remembered that the old man's eyes pained him in a strong light, but after the contrast of the light on the landing, the bedroom was dark, the shaded gas jet only giving enough light to show its own green shade.

"What a shambles!" thought the doctor as he swung the curtain back. The room was in an indescribable state, the bedclothes trailing across the floor from the gloomy four-poster, wash basin and crockery dragged down, the air foul and nauseating. "The poor old devil dragged himself along on the floor and reached for anything that gave him purchase," he thought. He snatched at the blankets and hurried back to the landing, where Virgilia knelt beside her father, chafing his hands.

"Wrap him in these and then fill some hot-water bottles," said Longaby. "I won't be a minute."

"Can't we get him into bed?" she asked. "He's so cold."

"I'm sorry, but it would be wasted effort," he replied. "I shall ring for an ambulance and have him taken to hospital." He heard her protest, but he hurried away. Longaby knew quite well that Adrian Delafield had had some sort of stroke, probably a cerebral hæmorrhage, and that he would probably never speak or move again.

"God, what a mess!" he thought. "Ought I to have interfered before? But that woman was healthy enough, and she wasn't mad in a clinical sense—only plain bats."

But he remembered to go round the house and ascertain that all the doors were bolted before he went outside.

2

It was at the house next door but one that Longaby found a telephone, and thankfully called up the police and the Infirmary. Here, at the Villa Magnolia, lived Carlotta d'Este and her daughter. Carlotta was a retired opera singer, stout, practical, exuberant.

"It was only a matter of time before something happened there," she said positively. "That woman—the Trimming—she gave me the horrors. Poor old man! The daughter should not have allowed it to go on. But never expect common sense or humanity from an academic woman. All those brains..."

Longaby did not wait to argue; he was beginning to feel exasperated. He wanted to shout back, "The Trimming has looked after the old chap for donkey's years and she did it damn' well. She kept him clean and warm, and well fed and happy, and it's not my fault she fell downstairs, anybody can fall downstairs."

He rushed back to Firenze, aware of all the patients who were in need of him—pneumonias, duodenals, expectant mothers, bronchitics, arthritics, asthmatics—he could do something for all of them, and nothing at all for Trimming and damn' little for Adrian Delafield.

He had left the front gate of Firenze open, so that the police and the ambulance men could get in, and he found a gaping group of staring people round the gate. It was always the same, he pondered. You wanted somebody to lend a hand and the street was invariably empty; you discovered a disaster and people collected from nowhere.

"Has she done him in, Doctor?" demanded a ghoulish old woman whose face Longaby remembered somehow. "I always said it'd happen some time. Talk of hell..."

He pushed her aside and hurried upstairs. Virgilia had recovered her normal calm, but her face was nearly as grey as her hair. "He's very ill," she said, and glanced up at Longaby.

"Yes. I'm afraid he won't get better, Miss Delafield. He's a great age."

"I know, but I'm sorry it happened like this," she said. "Perhaps I ought to have insisted on different arrangements, but it was all so difficult."

"I was as much responsible as you," he said quietly. "In my judgment, there was no need for apprehension. Trimming was able bodied and competent, and she was not mad—not as an alienist would use the word." He broke off as he heard steps approaching the front door. "That will be the ambulance men and the police. Will you go back to the studio and wait till I come? There's nothing you can do here. I will see to everything. You've had a bad shock and it will be better for you to rest before you answer the inevitable questions."

"Very well. I will do as you suggest," she replied. "I admit I feel confused and upset, but I shall be ready when you need me."

3

Inspector John Dowding, of D Division, took in the essentials of the layout in a very short time. Firenze was a detached house, standing in about half an acre of garden, surrounded by a six-foot wall. It fronted eastwards on to Laburnum Road, the front door being about thirty feet from the road. There was a wide hall, which went from back to front of the house, and on the west side was the Gothic doorway which gave on to the covered way leading to the studio. On the south side was the big drawing-room, opening on to the terrace, and the kitchens were on the north, dining-room and library being in the north-west and south-west corners respectively. The studio had its own door in the wall which surrounded the property (Dowding, of course, knew the neighbourhood well), and the studio entrance gave on to a cul-de-sac, where stables had been converted to lock-up garages.

At Longaby's request, Dowding went upstairs first and was told how the old man had been lying when he was found.

"What sort of condition was he in?" asked the inspector. "Was he paralysed, or could he walk?"

"He wasn't paralysed. He could stand up, and he could walk with assistance," replied Longaby. "So far as I can make out, Trimming kept him in bed permanently at one time—he was probably less trouble that way. Then when Miss Delafield insisted on a doctor seeing him regularly, Mareston told Trimming to get him up into a chair for a few hours every day. He hadn't been downstairs for some time, and his leg muscles had gone."

"So you think it's only to be expected he'd have fallen down if he'd got nobody to help him?"

"Yes. Also, you've got to remember he'd have been frightened out of his wits. He'd have heard the crash as Trimming fell. Of course we don't know how long it was before he made up his mind to try to get downstairs. He may have dithered for hours and then got panic stricken at being alone."

"Any chance of his being able to tell us?"

"None whatever, I should think. The only surprising thing is that he's alive at all. Can these chaps get him on the stretcher now?"

"Yes. I'll go and consider the other one—no hurry about her," replied Dowding.

It was about five minutes before Longaby returned to the inspector, the ambulance having moved off with the stretcher case. Dowding was standing by the drawing-room door, staring in at the mess of fallen plaster.

"Any opinion about all this?" he asked Longaby, and the latter shrugged his shoulders.

"Only the obvious one. There had been a chap doing repairs to the ceiling—not before it was needed. My guess is that the plaster cornice fell just as Trimming was fetching the old man's supper tray. The noise gave her a nasty turn and she tried to rush downstairs and tripped over that stair rod and the loose drugget. I've noticed those stair rods—the screw holes are loose and they shift, and once the drugget moves, it's a menace. The fact she'd got the tray in her hands made things worse, she just pitched from top to bottom."

"Looks like it," said Dowding. He nodded towards the fallen plaster. "There's a clock in there—it must have been on the mantelpiece and the plaster hit it. It stopped at three minutes to nine. The watch Trimming was wearing—a great turnip of a thing—stopped two minutes later."

"I reckoned it was all of twelve hours since she died," said Longaby. "Actually, it was a bit more—but I was near enough."

Dowding nodded. "Do you know anything about the work that was being done in here?"

"Not at first hand. You'd better ask Miss Delafield. And if I can take you in to see her, I could then get on with my rounds—before any other patients fall downstairs or have heart attacks because I'm late."

"Right," said Dowding. "I'll come along now and the photographers can do their stuff here. I like to have a record, even in a case like this which looks straightforward." He moved towards the Gothic doorway, adding: "I'd be glad if you'd give me an opinion on the deceased. Just how mad was she?"

"Kindly remember I've only seen her twice," said Longaby. "Mareston looked after this case until he crocked up. In my opinion, Trimming was not mad; that is to say, she was not certifiable. She was an exhibitionist and an eccentric, and she'd got a swarm of bees in her bonnet about religious topics; but she was not mad."

"Well, I'm interested to have your opinion about her," said Dowding. "As you probably know, she's a legend in this neighbourhood."

"I've no doubt she is," replied Longaby, "but anybody who has lived in this neighbourhood for long (which I have not) can tell you that Trimming has run this house single-handed for years. She has done the cleaning and cooking and shopping, kept the household accounts, given the old man his medicines, all without making a mess of things. She wasn't mad at all, barring her exhibitionism, and there was method in her simulated madness."

"Meaning that her peculiarities were calculated to keeping her in the position of boss?" inquired Dowding.

"Yes. She was in a strong position, you know. She managed the show very competently, and she was obviously an impossible person to live with. She'd certainly have driven anybody else mad if they'd tried to live in the same house with her."

Dowding nodded and paused a moment by the wrought-iron gate, looking across the grass to the Florentine well-head.

"It might be anywhere," he said. "I've only been in Italy once, but if there were a few Judas trees making a wallop of magenta, instead of lilac and laburnum—well, it'd pass for Tuscany."

"Quite true," agreed Longaby; "but you can stare when I've gone. I've got about twenty patients to see before one o'clock surgery."

"Sorry, Doc," said Dowding. "Just one question before you go. You were first on the spot. Was there a single thing which made you wonder if deceased really *had* fallen downstairs, alone and unaided?"

Longaby took his time over answering, for all his desire to be off. When he did answer it was with decision.

"Not a thing," he replied. "And there was this: the front and back doors and the kitchen door were all bolted inside; the shutters I smashed in had got their bar in position. And if you find a single window unlatched I shall be surprised."

"The old man's bedroom window was open," said Dowding.

"Because Miss Delafield opened it. If you had smelt the room when we went into it, you wouldn't have blamed her."

"O.K.," said Dowding. "I'll let you know about the inquest. And now just come and introduce me to Miss Delafield; I like to be polite when circumstances permit."

"Very nice, but you might remember she's had the hell of a shock and she's not the world's chicken," said Longaby, "so if she's not as precise as you'd like, don't bully her. She's a decent old scout in her bookish way."

V

I

INSPECTOR JOHN DOWDING WAS BY NO MEANS DEVOID OF imagination and his experience of the world was much wider than that of most pre-war policemen. He had served in the army from 1939 to 1945, and his service had taken him to Italy; he had been in Rome and Florence, in Milan, Siena and Perugia, and having been given a good secondary education by his hardworking parents, he had enough background to appreciate what he'd seen. He had chosen the police force as a career because he believed that a determined fellow could climb the police ladder fairly quickly in post-war conditions, and because he was intelligent, hard working and observant he was well on his way towards the sort of position he wanted. Dowding had been in D Division for five years and during that time he had heard the local rumours about Trimming, and even seen her tall black-cloaked figure hurrying silently to the shops. (The tradesmen did not ever suggest that Trimming was mad; she was a good shopper and she always counted her change.) Dowding knew the outside of the Delafield studio by sight—as much as could be seen of it above the wall which enclosed the property—and he had been told that the studio was hung with the old painter's canvases, but when he first entered the studio, he felt (like the Queen of Sheba) "the half was not told him."

Dr. Longaby introduced him to Virgilia Delafield with decorum, and Dowding saw a neat sturdy figure in a well-cut suit, with neatly-cropped grey hair and intelligent grey eyes studying him through dark horn-rimmed spectacles. But behind and around that reticent figure were the pictures, frame touching gold frame, an orgy of bright colours, romantic figures and eyes which followed you round.

"Good morning, Inspector," said Virgilia. "Don't take any notice of the pictures. You get used to them after a while."

It was the oddest greeting Dowding had ever received during his period as a policeman, but Longaby didn't seem to think it peculiar. He only said:

"Well, I'll be getting on with my round, Inspector." He then turned to Miss Delafield. "I'll look in later. Take things quietly and try not to worry." With a nod to Dowding, he hurried off, and the inspector said:

"I'm sorry you've had all this distress, madam. Do you feel able to answer a few questions?"

"Of course," said Virgilia. "Don't think because I'm elderly I am of necessity feeble. I admit I was upset—so would anybody have been—but I'm perfectly all right now. I shall be very glad to answer your questions. I can imagine there's a fine old crop of rumours going round."

Her voice was tart and clear, and Dowding felt relieved. He knew a promising witness when he met one.

"First, about the deceased, madam—Miss Trimming. Could I have her full name?"

"I don't know her full name. I never heard my father call her anything but Trimming," she replied, "and I've never had any reason to inquire. If that sounds odd to you, may I explain what I do know in my own words? I've been trying to think things out, but I'm afraid I can't be so helpful as I should like to be."

Dowding agreed at once, and Virgilia spoke with clear deliberation. "Trimming came to the house in 1920. Previous to that date there were two servants, a married couple named Long; they were both elderly and Trimming came to help Mrs. Long in the kitchen. I did not live here; I have never lived here until the last nine months, but I remember when I asked my father where he had found this extraordinary-looking servant—Trimming was extraordinary even then—I think he replied he had got her from an orphanage run by a Protestant community. I believe Mrs. Long died about 1930, and I gather my father was not then making the big income he made in his younger days, and Trimming ran the household single-handed, with a gardener and odd-job man who came in daily." She paused, and then added: "I'm sorry if I'm being slow, and perhaps verbose, but it isn't easy to remember things all that time ago, especially as I never lived here."

Dowding reassured her, and she went on: "Then my father bought a house outside Paris, and I think he often shut this house up for months at a time and lived in Passy, Trimming going there with him. I do know that in 1940, when France fell, he was in Passy, and I understand that it was due to Trimming's efforts he got back to England. I was in Canada during the war, and an old friend of my father's—a Mr. Lestrange—wrote and told me that Father was safely back here." She paused a moment, and then went on: "I have told you all that rigmarole, Inspector, to make you understand that Trimming was in a privileged position—my father relied on her more and more. Well, when I finally came back to England nine months ago, I came here to see my father and Trimming told me he was not well and did not wish to see anybody. It all seemed most peculiar. I went in to see one or two of the elder tradespeople—none of whom knew me—and mentioned where I was staying, and the next day I received an anonymous letter hinting that my father was dead. I have found later that a number of people believed he was dead. Since I believe the police are very meticulous in their records, you probably know that I enlisted the assistance of a constable on the beat in order to gain admission here to see my own father."

"Yes, madam; the fact was reported," replied Dowding.

"Very good. I found no horrors, no scandals. The house was well cared for, my father well looked after, but he had been persuaded to remain in bed permanently, and I think he was frightened. You probably know the rest of the story. I insisted that a doctor should see my father regularly and I put a stop to the visits of some eccentric minister of religion introduced by Trimming."

"One question here, madam," said Dowding, interrupting for the first time. "Can you tell me the minister's name, or anything else about him?"

"I'm sorry, but I'm afraid I can't," she replied. "I only saw him once, and took an intense dislike to him. He was what I should call a semi-literate fanatic—like one of the local preachers who rant at revival meetings. My father called him Habbakuk, but it's improbable that that was the creature's name. However, the point was that he terrified my father. With my father's consent, I decided to come and live in the studio here; it seemed to me that I could then supervise the ménage to some extent, without disrupting it."

"You certainly did your best to see that your father was looked after," said Dowding, but Virgilia snapped back at him:

"And everything I did was futile—I recognise that now. But if I had insisted on living in the house, Trimming would have left—she told me so. And whatever her eccentricities and abnormalities, she did look after my father and keep him well and happy in his own home."

"Thank you very much for telling me about everything so clearly," said Dowding. "You probably know that the law requires a full description of any person on whom an inquest is held. The coroner will ask for a Christian name and will expect the police to find next of kin of deceased—if such exist."

"Next of kin—to Trimming?" pondered Virgilia. "I've never heard of any kin at all. I'm sure my father didn't know of any. And as for a Christian name, if the coroner demands a label I suggest Martha. My father did sometimes speak of Trimming as Martha. But you may find some evidence of origin among her belongings. I've never been up to her bedroom, so I've no idea what's there."

Dowding was an observant man. He noticed Miss Delafield's use of the word "may" and he believed she had used it deliberately. Getting more and more interested in what he had known to be "an odd set-up," he inquired: "Have you anything to add to that, madam?"

"Only that I have sometimes wondered if Trimming were illiterate—using the word in its exact meaning," she said. "I am a great believer in written instructions—saves argument. But when I typed out a few lines for Trimming, she always insisted on my repeating my instructions verbally."

"I see," said Dowding. "Would you say that her intelligence was sub-normal?"

"Certainly not. She was acutely intelligent; she had a most retentive memory, she could add up and reckon correctly and she had an extensive if peculiar vocabulary. I may be quite wrong in my surmise."

"Everybody around here regarded her as very strange," said Dowding. "Now, finally, madam, Dr. Longaby mentioned that there had been a man doing repairs to the drawing-room ceiling. Can you tell me his name, or the firm which sent him?"

"His name was Walter—or so my father called him," she replied. "Presumably he came from the builder's in the High Street. I shall have to explain again about the conditions under which I have lived here. I never interfered with Trimming in her management of the house. When I observed that the drawing-room ceiling was in a dangerous state, I told my father about it—he had days when he was quite practical and collected. He agreed at once that repairs should be put in hand and I heard him tell Trimming to give orders to the builders to that effect. A few days later a man was working on the ceiling and my father said, 'Walter is doing that ceiling.' I went in to see what was being done, but did not interfere in any way. I never interfered unless it was absolutely necessary."

"Quite so," said Dowding. "Now was the man still working here yesterday?"

"No. I understand he finished the job the day before yesterday—Tuesday," replied Virgilia. "Presumably he was inefficient and the weight of the new plaster brought the cornice down, or something of that kind."

Dowding nodded. "I shall have to find out about him," he said, "also to determine if anything is missing from the house. Could you tell me if there was an inventory of the contents?"

"I've no idea," she replied. "How could I have? I deliberately refrained from asking any questions of that kind. If once Trimming had thought I was being suspicious—or making my father suspicious—there would have been unending trouble."

"I want you to understand all the points which have to be considered in this matter, madam," said Dowding. "The police cannot afford to take anything for granted. At first sight it seems obvious that Miss Trimming fell downstairs, having been startled, perhaps, by the crash of the falling plaster. But there is no proof that she fell downstairs of her own volition, nor yet that it was the falling plaster which startled her into losing her footing."

"Yes, yes. Don't imagine I can't follow a plain argument," said Virgilia tersely. "You are envisaging a robbery and all that that implies. But I should imagine that the police are well equipped to recognise any sign of housebreakers. I take it that you have been round the house?"

"I have only had time for a quick glance round," said Dowding. "I understand from Dr. Longaby that the front door and the door leading to the covered way were both bolted on the inside and the back door was both bolted and chained."

"Have you examined the window catches?" demanded Virgilia.

"Not yet," replied Dowding.

"Then may I suggest you go and do so?" she replied with some asperity. "It seems unprofitable to elaborate a hypothesis if the basic assumption be incorrect. I shall be quite prepared to come round the house with you, or give you my opinion (for what it is worth) as to whether anything is missing once you have established the probability of breaking and entering, as I believe it is called."

With surprising meekness, Dowding agreed. He began to realise that Miss Virgilia Delafield could conceivably be a proper terror.

2

When the inspector re-entered the house, he found the police surgeon brooding over Trimming's body. The photographers had finished their job in the hall, and the body had been moved.

Trimming now lay on her back, her startled eyes staring up at the ceiling, her mouth open, as though she had given a final scream before hitting the floor. Dr. Glossop (the police surgeon) nodded to Dowding.

"I don't see anything against it," he said. "Appearances are quite consistent with the woman having started to rush downstairs with the tray in her hands, caught her toe in the drugget where it's ruckled up and pitched right forward on her head at the bottom. Apparently the old chap had had his supper—chicken soup, fried fillets of sole and a savoury *soufflé* to follow. Very nice, too. There was a milk drink in addition, well whisked. He hadn't finished that. You can see some of it on the stairs where she first stumbled, as though the glass were jerked up. The cat's lapped up what went on the tiles down here. Well, it looks reasonable enough to me, but the result would have been the same if anybody tripped her up or grabbed her ankle."

Dowding nodded. "O.K., Doc. I know you'll go over her with care."

"Then I'll tell the chaps to shift her. Rum looking customer," replied Glossop.

Dowding then went over the house, with particular attention to the windows. With the exception of Adrian Delafield's bedroom (where the bottom of the window was wide open) all the windows were latched and there was evidence to show that they had not been opened for some time. Only two bedrooms were in use—the large one used by Delafield, and a small one (which had been intended for a dressing-room) on the same floor, used by Trimming. It was a bare, comfortless little room: linoleum on the floor, a narrow iron bedstead with a hard flock mattress, two grey blankets and old cotton sheets, a small washstand and a tiny cheap-looking glass. A yellow-painted chest-of-drawers contained a minimum of old-fashioned underclothes and a curtain across a corner hid another black serge frock and a long black coat. There was a Bible beside the bed, and remembering Miss Delafield's suggestion, Dowding studied it. If Trimming had had a Bible, presumably she must have read it; it was full of markers—most of them texts or pictures—but the markers seemed to have been put in to keep the place of favourite pictures. It was an illustrated Bible, full of pictures of German origin. On the wall hung two primitive colour prints, a "Rock of Ages" with a presumably drowning female in a stormy sea, and a Christian martyr effect with a large proportion of lions to Christians. There were no letters or papers or documents of any kind in the room.

Dowding stood for a moment and considered. There were six bedrooms in the house altogether. Although not in use, they were well furnished, with good old-fashioned beds, carpets, mats, easy chairs and everything that went to the furnishing of a comfortable—if dated—bedroom. There were linen cupboards and well-stocked blanket boxes—all reeking of moth balls. "I suppose there are people like that," he mused, "making a virtue of discomfort."

He went down to the drawing-room, where a bored constable surveyed the heap of fallen plaster. One thing at least was plain—the window and shutters had been secured, because Longaby had had his work cut out to break in; and the footmarks of two people and two people only, showed on the dusty floor. The footprints continued across the hall, showing where Longaby and Virgilia Delafield had walked. The furniture was pushed to one side of the room and was covered in dust sheets. A door gave on to a smaller room, and here Dowding found that pictures and ornaments were stacked. He got the impression that the drawing-room had been cleaned after the plastering was finished, and that the pictures and ornaments and china had also been cleaned ready to put back where they belonged. There was one cabinet in the drawing-room where china and silver were back in place.

Dowding went from room to room—dining-room, shuttered and dark, full of heavy mahogany furniture. Pulling out a drawer he found silver spoons and forks and knives stacked in tidy rows under green baize covers, and other table silver—solid at that—in cases. It was the kitchens which interested Dowding most: the gas jets were alight in kitchen and scullery, the kitchen boiler still warm. The kitchens were stone-floored, inconvenient and hideous with old-fashioned paper on the walls, but they were neat and clean. The china used by Trimming for her own supper was stacked in the sink—she had had a cup of cocoa and bread and dripping. As the inspector stood and stared the big black cat came and miaowed at him, and on impulse he gave it some milk which he found in a saucepan. It seemed a very orderly household in its dated way, but Dowding had an odd sense of being watched as he stood by the old-fashioned sink and looked at the china which Trimming had meant to wash up.

3

"So far as I can tell, nothing is missing, Inspector," said Virgilia Delafield. "Admittedly, I am no authority on my father's bric-à-brac, but everything I remember seems to be here. I doubt if it would be worth anybody's while to take it away—except for the table silver, and all that is there." She turned to him rather wearily. "You tell me that all the doors and windows were secured and that there is no sign of anybody breaking in. Isn't that sufficient evidence that nobody did break in?"

"Yes, madam, but I am thinking of the man who did the plastering. Nobody in the High Street knows anything about him; he doesn't seem to have been a local workman."

"What does it matter?" she snapped. "My father knew who he was. Admittedly, I thought he was next door to a mental defective, but he finished working here the day before yesterday, and I am quite certain that Trimming was satisfied that there had been no petty larceny. And if you are assuming that he got into the house for illicit purposes, how do you assume he got out again?"

"I am not assuming anything, madam," replied Dowding, who was getting a bit tired of being treated as the dull boy of the class. "My duty is to get all the relevant facts to put before the coroner. Now, would you tell me where Mr. Delafield would keep his business papers—bank statements and so forth."

"Presumably in his bedroom, since he hardly ever left it," she replied. "You'd better look for yourself; not that there will be much to find. He owns the house, and the deeds will be at the bank, also securities—if he's got any. He told me that he put all his savings into an annuity some years back—the most sensible thing he could do. Trimming did the housekeeping; I think she went to the bank and changed a cheque once a week, and she doubtless accounted for it to my father in her own peculiar way. I made no inquiries—it wasn't my business."

"There are no papers or letters of any kind in Miss Trimming's room, not even a National Insurance card," said Dowding. "Yet, presumably she had one, being an employed person."

"I can't tell you anything about that," replied Virgilia. "It's to be supposed that my father paid her a salary, but I can't tell you how much."

"It's very odd," said Dowding slowly. "I have looked carefully through her room and through the kitchen drawers, and I can find no savings bank-book, no money put away, no notes on spending or saving."

"She probably didn't make any," replied Miss Delafield. "I've never seen her put pen to paper. She could count and add, but she did it on her fingers. I think you'll probably find the household bills somewhere. She paid cash for everything, but always asked for a bill and gave it to my father. He said she was very careful, and I know he trusted her with everything."

She broke off and looked at Dowding with an expression of exasperation. "Don't tell me again that you find it's all very odd," she said. "Nobody knows it better than I do. In my opinion Trimming was quite mad. I've said so to everybody who was concerned. I told both the doctors so, but they agreed with me that Trimming's form of madness did not prevent her looking after my father very well indeed, provided there was enough supervision to prevent her bullying him. As to her savings, if any, I expect she hid them under a floorboard, or in a chimney, or perhaps buried in a pot in the garden, like a French peasant. And what does it matter, anyway? There's nobody to claim her savings, and I hope you don't think I'm interested—because I'm not."

"I'm very sorry, madam," said Dowding. He spoke soberly and sincerely, for he was a very decent fellow. "I realise that all this inquiry is very tiresome for you, and that you have suffered a shock in finding your father as you did. The last thing I want to do is to bother you further than is necessary in the circumstances."

"Don't think I'm blaming you, Inspector," replied Virgilia. "You have been most considerate and efficient, but do remember this: this household has been notorious for its eccentricity for years. Nothing that I say about Trimming is harsh in comparison with the stories invented about her in the neighbourhood. As a police officer, you must have heard some of the rumours. I came here to live, not at my own wish, but because I considered it my duty, and I called in such supervision as seemed desirable. Granted the circumstances, are you surprised that things seem a little odd? Really, if you had found me stark mad with straws in my hair it wouldn't have been in the least surprising."

Dowding smiled back at her. "Yes, madam. All you say is perfectly reasonable, and I respect you for your restraint. You have said 'I don't know' when that was the case, and very few witnesses are as clear-headed as you have been."

"Thank you for the kind words," said Virgilia. "And now, am I allowed to go to the hospital and see my father? It may be a futile errand, but it's all I can do. I wanted him to live out his life in his own home and to die peacefully in his own bed. It hasn't happened that way, but I should like to go to see him."

"Of course," said Dowding. He felt it was all he could say, but Virgilia had the last word.

"And you can look through the studio if you like. I only beg that if you must read my notes on Calvinism, you will leave them as you find them."

VI

I

"WELL, I DON'T KNOW..." SAID JOCELYN TRUBY.

"That's part of the fun," said a girl's voice behind him. "If you just don't know, you never get tired of it. Every day it can be something different."

"But I like to know where I am," said Jocelyn.

Mr. Truby was at another art exhibition. It was strikingly different from that of the Great Victorians which he had visited with Susan a few weeks back. The present show was being held in Peter Raven's flat. The mews flat made a very charming setting for the exhibits; it had once been a stable, and consisted mainly of one long room whose white walls were distinguished because the brickwork had not been plastered over, and the consequent rough surface had a pleasant diapered effect. A low shelf, or projection, ran the full length of the room, from a modern window at one end to the corner where Peter's divan (neatly tailored) was pushed against the far wall, and on this shelf stood a dozen or so canvases and panels which, together with a few mobiles, constituted the exhibition. Two of the canvases were Susan's, and Jocelyn was wondering what he could do with them if he bought them, for he was very fond of his niece. He was beginning to understand Susan's preoccupation with Peter Raven. Jocelyn was not sure if he liked Peter himself, but it was certainly useful to know a young man who could convert his flat into a picture gallery.

"It looks terribly nice in this room, doesn't it?" put in the girl's voice, and Jocelyn turned round to her with a chuckle. This was Jill Grantham, Susan's great friend.

"And are you suggesting that I should buy a picture in order to endow this room with it in perpetuity?" he asked.

"It'd be a noble gesture," said Jill. "Nice for Susan to sell a picture and nice for Peter to possess it. He's been terribly magnanimous in lending us his flat. Oh, hallo, how nice of you to come!"

She turned towards a big shaggy fellow, older than the majority of the visitors, and said:

"Do you know Max Baring, Mr. Truby? He's an art critic."

"God bless my soul, I've know him since you were in pinafores," said Jocelyn, and Jill replied:

"Isn't that lovely! Max can tell you that Susan's painting really has got something…"

She slid away and Jocelyn looked at Max's square, lined face. "Has it?" he asked.

Max looked at the indeterminate canvas with its shimmer of weeping willow greens and harsh black lines. "Not really. Pretty enough, but derived. She'd much better get married. By the way, didn't I hear you talking about old Adrian Delafield the other day? Have you heard the sad story about him?"

"Delafield? It's only a week or so since I saw him. What's the trouble?"

"He's in hospital—on his last legs, I gather. It's a grim story. Come and sit on that chap's bed—if it is his bed. It's quieter over there."

Jocelyn followed Baring's sturdy figure down the long room and they perched on the divan in the corner and Max Baring said: "The housekeeper—a character named Trimming—took a toss down the stairs one evening and broke her neck. She wasn't found until the doctor came next morning, and poor old Delafield seems to have tried to get to her and fallen downstairs in his turn. He's had a stroke or something. It's a curious story…"

While the cheerful party jostled to and fro in front of the exhibits, talking ever more loudly and treading cigarette ends into Peter Raven's carpet, Max Baring rumbled on about the accident at Firenze, and Jocelyn tut-tutted in deep concern. Then it was Jocelyn's turn to dispense information and Max was just saying:

"Why not give the local police a ring? They're very stuck for information—inquest this morning; it was adjourned. Means they're not satisfied, you know."

"But I don't really *know* anything, not more than the police themselves would know," said Jocelyn. "Still, I'll think about it. Poor old chap."

"Do you smoke, Mr. Truby?"

Peter Raven stood with a large box of superior cigarettes encouragingly displayed and Jocelyn had time to think, "Very generous of him to provide cigarettes for all this crowd" before he replied: "Not for me, thank you very much. But Baring smokes. Do you know one another?"

Max Baring tilted his head up and up until he could see Peter's intelligent face—his height always startled the average-sized person—and then exclaimed:

"Why, by gad! I saw you the other evening, at that pub—the Blenheim Arms. Are you a denizen of St. John's Wood?"

"No. I live here. That's my bed," rejoined Peter.

"But you were at the Blenheim the other night, when they were discussing Adrian Delafield and his housekeeper?" insisted Baring.

"Yes. I dropped in for a drink," agreed Peter. "It was rather a pleasant pub—like a village local." He turned back to Truby.

"What do you think of the products of the younger generation, sir?"

"I feel rather like you felt when you had a glimpse of Adrian Delafield's studio the other day," replied Jocelyn. "You said, 'It can't be true.'"

"Ah, you've been there, have you?" said Baring. "Have you heard about the old man's accident?"

"Somebody told me the incredible housekeeper had fallen downstairs and broken her neck," replied Peter; "but I rather discounted it as exaggeration. Everybody tends to exaggerate when they talk about Delafield. Susan would say it's because his pictures are so large and so many."

"Whose pictures?" asked Susan. She was looking very *soignée* in a steel-blue grosgrain coat with white ruffles at the neck and Peter smiled at her, his smile almost a caress.

"Old Delafield's," he replied. "Too much and too many. I just can't forget that studio. It's a jungle in paint, proliferating—"

"You mean prolific," snapped Truby. "Pictures don't proliferate. Susan, my dear, I'm very upset. Poor old Delafield's in hospital and Trimming's broken her neck."

"Trimming? Oh, surely not! And I never even saw her," said Susan. "I'm so sorry, Jocelyn. However did it happen?"

"She fell downstairs with the supper tray," said Max. "I don't want to be callous, but she'd have made a wonderful corpse—with the supper all scattered."

"*Nature morte*," murmured Peter, but Susan put in severely:

"I think you're being most unsympathetic. Jocelyn, did poor old Mr. Delafield fall downstairs, too?"

"Yes. He tried to get to Trimming. It's a most melancholy story," said Truby. "I think I shall go and see Miss Virgilia; it's a wretched business for her. Inquests are always most upsetting. I wonder if she's got anybody to help her. Is that nephew of hers about, Susan?"

"Roy? No, I don't think he is. He was taking some American plutocrats to Provence or somewhere. Do go and see Miss Virgilia, Jocelyn. She'll love to talk to you; she's terribly fond of her father."

"Why, you all seem to know the household," said Max. "I envy you. I've often wanted to get a peep at that studio myself. It's pure *Edouard Sept,* I'm told."

"You do a nice write-up of our show and I'll try to get you a private view of the Delafield studio," said Susan shamelessly. "Jocelyn, dear, if you really want to go to see Miss Virgilia, I'm sure Peter would drive you—and then I can come too, with a nice bunch of flowers and kind inquiries. I really did like her. She was so sensible and kind and practical, living amongst all those perfectly dreadful pictures."

"Very thoughtful of you, my dear, but I think it'd be better if I went by myself. If she wants to talk, or perhaps ask a word of advice on the legal side, it'd be easier for her if we were alone. And Mr. Raven should stay here and keep his eye on things. At affairs like this, pilfering is all too easy."

"I don't think there's much to pilfer, but need you call him Mr. Raven?" said Susan. "It sounds so improbable. I've never known him as anything but Peter."

"It was old Barrie who was responsible for the crop of Peters," said Jocelyn unkindly. "Peter and Wendy were at the peak of their popularity just about thirty years ago. Max probably derives from the Anthony Hope period, twenty years earlier."

Max Baring grinned. "Too true. And Jocelyn is a hangover from Arthurian romance and Alfred, Lord Tennyson. Well, if you're not accepting a lift in that lethal-looking outfit outside the window, I'll see you to the Tube. Or are you buying a picture before you go?"

"I'll look in later, if I may. I don't want to discourage other buyers," said Jocelyn. He nodded to Peter. "May I say that I think it was very generous of you to lend your abode for an affair of this kind? Very handsome, indeed."

"Peter's a very kind-hearted person," said Susan. "Give my love to Miss Virgilia and tell her how sorry I am, Jocelyn."

2

"No, Mr. Truby. I have not told the police; I can see no object in telling them. It would only add to the fuss, and there has been fuss enough already. I cannot tell you how wearisome and distasteful the whole business has been. The very last thing I wish to do is to give fresh grounds for futile inquiry."

Virgilia Delafield spoke trenchantly, but her elderly face was strained and weary, and kind old Jocelyn Truby felt it was almost brutal to argue with her. Nevertheless, he was a very conscientious man with a strong sense of law and order, and he felt it incumbent on him to make his point.

"My dear lady, I fully realise and sympathise with your distress," he said; "but it seems plain that the police have grounds for suspicion concerning this man who repaired the ceiling."

"Who destroyed the ceiling seems more accurate," she retorted acidly. "The man was a fool, a half-wit, I knew it at a glance. The police are making a fuss because they can't trace him. I have told them that my father sometimes employed the oddest people; he preferred to employ the sons or grandsons of tradesmen or craftsmen who worked for him long ago. I have been racking my brains to remember the name of the builder who put up the covered way. It's quite likely that this plasterer was connected with them. But I can't remember. And what *does* it matter, anyway?"

"It matters to this extent: that you had a mishap which might have been a dangerous accident when the board fell on you," said Jocelyn Truby.

"Fiddlesticks!" she snapped. "He left his gear badly balanced because he was incompetent: his work shows that, it was abominably done. If I had any suspicions at all about that incident, I should be disposed to believe that Trimming so arranged things that I should get a black eye. How she hated me, poor soul!"

"Of course, that is a possible explanation," agreed Truby. "But I find it very disquieting that this man cannot be traced."

"If he reads the account of the inquest, I should think he will be more than ever careful to keep out of the way," she replied. "If it became known that a whole ceiling collapsed because he 'repaired' a section of it, it would hardly be a good advertisement for him. I suggested to the police that we should learn whom he was when he sends his bill in; but I should think it's highly improbable he ever will send a bill now. I shouldn't, in the same circumstances."

Virgilia sat back in her chair and studied Jocelyn Truby's face with that acute analytical glance of hers.

"It is exceedingly kind of you to bother about all this," she added. "Don't think I'm ungrateful, I'm not. But when you express 'disquiet,' could you tell me exactly what it is that's bothering you?"

"Why, yes," declared Jocelyn. "It is this: there has been a workman in the house who was so incompetent that his work caused considerable damage, to say nothing of one accident which might have had serious results and another which ended in tragedy. This workman cannot be traced. It seems to me at least conceivable that the man was a scoundrel—even a criminal. He may have obtained access to the house with the intention of stealing. He may even have attacked Trimming when she came hurrying downstairs, as she undoubtedly would have done when she heard the ceiling collapse. I think it almost certain that the police envisage this possibility."

"Of course they do," she replied patiently. "It's the business of the police to 'envisage' all contingencies; it's what they are paid for. Now let us take your two points. As I see it, they are clear. First, the workman was a criminal. I will grant your premise, though I consider it improbable. Having robbed the house and hurled Trimming downstairs (it seems a redundant effort—he could have waited until she was in bed and asleep), he then left the house with his loot. Can you tell me exactly how he got out of the house? Because the police cannot."

"There must be many possibilities of egress," began Jocelyn cautiously, and she snapped back:

"There are doors—three of them to be precise—windows, twenty in all, a trapdoor to the roof and a hatch to the coal cellar. It was, perhaps, fortunate for me that Dr. Longaby entered the house with me. No one has suggested that he is in league with a hypothetical criminal, as far as I know. He found all three outside doors not only bolted but also chained. The ground floor windows were either shuttered or barred. The upstairs windows were latched—all of them. Admittedly, I opened the bedroom window, and I know that that also was securely latched. If you had experienced the atmosphere of the room you would have understood why I opened it."

"But of course," put in Jocelyn hastily, but she went on inexorably:

"This was one of the few occasions in my life when I thought I should be sick—so I opened the window. The police examined the trap to the roof and the coal hatch; both were bolted. Trimming was a careful soul, I will say that for her. She made it as difficult as possible for a burglar to break in and virtually impossible for one to get out without leaving evidence of 'egress,' if I may adopt your word."

"I see," said Jocelyn, and she laughed a little.

"My dear Mr. Truby, your theory won't work. But let us look at your second point—that of theft."

3

"In a sense it's a relief to talk things over in detail like this," said Virgilia. "I have only known you a short time, Mr. Truby, but I have enough perception to recognise integrity when I meet it, to say nothing of genuine kindness—and you did know my father. I have no hesitation in telling you the state of his affairs."

"I am very much honoured at your expression of confidence in me," said Jocelyn, and she went on:

"First, the possibility of theft. There was in that house no single article of great intrinsic value, so far as I know. There was a lot of nice china, some pleasant pottery and good glass, a few examples of Florentine goldsmiths' work (none of it missing), and a large collection of indifferent pictures. In addition there is a quantity of solid table silver, Georgian and Victorian. Thanks to Trimming's careful ways, it is plain that none of this has been stolen or even disturbed. I cannot see any reason to suspect theft of any household article, any curio or so called *objet d'art*. And that brings me to my father's finances. Since it is necessary for somebody to be in charge of his affairs (he will never be able to cope with them again, poor old father, even though he may live for some time), I have been given power of attorney by the bank and by his lawyer."

"Perfectly correct," murmured Jocelyn, and she added:

"He was put into a public ward in the Infirmary. I know it makes no difference to him where he is, but I have had him moved to a private room. It seemed to be the final indignity that he should die among paupers."

Jocelyn had a vein of sentiment in his make-up, and a not disinterested regard for the welfare of the aged, and he felt a tear pricking his eye. "I fully appreciate your feelings," he said.

Virgilia sniffed, and then as though ashamed of her concession to sentiment, added: "I know I'm illogical. When my turn comes I shall have no feeling about dying in a public ward; indeed, I shall probably be too poor to gain admission elsewhere. Which brings me back to the matter in hand."

She took a deep breath, and drew a pencil and paper towards her—she was sitting at her desk in a corner of the studio—as though note-making materials helped her to formulate her thoughts. "I had assumed—as doubtless others did—that my father was a wealthy man," she went on. "I knew that he made a lot of money at the peak of his career, and he was always reasonably provident—unlike many painters. I think it probable that he lost considerable capital during the war, but be that as it may, he has virtually no capital left. As he told me, he purchased an annuity. This brings in precisely ten pounds a week. That is what he lived on, assisted by Trimming's thrifty housekeeping. I have said many hard things about Trimming. I disliked her intensely—and vice versa—but I underestimated her good qualities. So far as I can gather, Trimming has received no wages for years; pocket money, perhaps, out of the housekeeping, but no real wages."

"But that's extraordinary," said Mr. Truby, and Virgilia nodded.

"It is indeed. I knew she was devoted to my father, and that she was almost fanatically attached to the house, but I had no notion of the real position." Taking up her pencil and making brief entries on her slip of paper, Virgilia went on: "My father's affairs are in perfect order—and extremely simple. The bank knows all about it. Each week, Trimming cashed my father's cheque for five pounds. Never more, never less. On that sum she kept house and paid for food, household necessaries and replacements. She paid for everything in cash and brought my father a sheaf of receipted bills each week. Coal, gas, rates and taxes were paid for by cheque out of his remaining five pounds a week. And there are no outstanding debts. It can be described as an excellent piece of domestic economy."

"It can indeed," said Jocelyn warmly. (He knew exactly how put to it he was himself to keep up a comfortable bachelor establishment in London on an invested income of £2,000 a year—all liable to taxation as unearned income.)

"Of course your father owns his house," he added, and again Miss Virgilia almost snapped back.

"Not at all. I thought he did. Everybody else thought he did, but he doesn't. He bought the last fifty years of a ninety-nine years' lease, and the lease expires in two years' time."

"Dear me," said Jocelyn weakly, and she echoed him: "Yes. Dear me. The lease, as was customary in the days when it was drawn up, gives the ground landlord the right to claim dilapidations. I wish the ground landlord joy of them. Certainly my father will not be alive to face the embarrassments of the situation, and his annuity dies with him. The only assets will be his furniture—and pictures."

There was irony in her voice as she raised her head and looked at the serried canvases, at Annunciation Angels and Red Cross Knights, at Minstrel Boys and Bold Lochinvar, at Savonarola and Cardinal Mazarin, at The Woman of Samaria and Ruth and Naomi, and a host of other highly recognisable historical or mythological characters.

"Serve the ground landlord right!" she declared. "I consider dilapidations an iniquitous system. Among other things, this studio and the covered way have to be demolished. Oh, I've no patience with any of it. And how thankful I am that I have no means save what I earn. I will go on Public Assistance before I earn a penny to reimburse the ground landlord for dilapidations."

"Hear, hear! I applaud your spirit!" cried Jocelyn, and he did. No tears from Virgilia. Her mention of "public assistance" demonstrated her determination.

"But... has he made a will?" asked Jocelyn anxiously, and for once Miss Virgilia chuckled.

"Happily, no," she replied. "Not so far as we can ascertain. I shall not be in the invidious position of inheriting the very fag-end of a Victorian lease. Presumably, my nephew, Roy Braithwaite, is the legal heir to his grandfather's property. I feel certain that his ingenuity will not be at a loss when it comes to declining such a formidable inheritance. He will probably bestow it on some public figure. I would suggest the Pope. The Vatican lawyers are well versed in legal controversy, and they are famous for never parting with property once vested in their Establishment."

"Dear me," said Jocelyn again, and after a glance at Miss Virgilia's face he allowed himself to laugh, and Virgilia laughed with him.

"I know the whole thing is a deplorable muddle," she said; "but crying won't help. There's one good point, and I can't be sufficiently thankful for it: my father's annuity will go on till he dies, and enable him to die in peace and privacy. But as for all this nonsense about the house being robbed and Trimming attacked—I've no patience with it. Father's income was a pretty tight fit, you know; if there had been anything valuable to sell, he'd have sold it long since. He was still remarkably on the spot so far as expenses were concerned—everything was perfectly in order."

"I thought him remarkably on the spot altogether," said Jocelyn. "His memory was surprising."

"I'm so glad you saw him!" she exclaimed. "The coroner and police had a tendency to speak of him as though he were completely senile. If the question arises, you can give evidence that he had his wits about him, even though he did drop off to sleep at unexpected moments."

"I certainly will," said Mr. Truby firmly.

VII

I

"WELL, THERE YOU ARE," SAID DOWDING. "WE'VE ALL had a bash at it. The D.D.I. chewed it over, the Divisional C.I.D. boys did their stuff, we've pestered you for odd details and we've just about worked ourselves to a standstill. But I'm not going to say I'm satisfied, because I'm not."

Dowding was talking to Inspector Lancing, C.I.D. The latter, having come from Scotland Yard to make an inquiry of his own in D Division's territory, had looked in at the police station in the High Street in a friendly informal sort of way, and inquired how the Trimming case was shaping. Both Lancing and his immediate superior, Chief Inspector Rivers, had taken a lively interest in Trimming's death: the more details they heard about her, the more intrigued they became. Trimming was a character with a big C, and Rivers liked characters, particularly those of riper years. He maintained that the young of to-day—particularly delinquent young—were all plagiarists; originality and genuine oddity pertained to those born at the turn of the century or earlier.

Lancing, for his part, was becoming quite a student of "home accidents." The number of fatal accidents which occurred during domestic occupations was steadily rising—the statistics of home accidents are quite as shocking as those of road accidents—and Lancing said that accidental deaths caused by falling downstairs, or falling off ladders, or out of windows, were of the "you never can tell" category. He and Dowding had already had a good heart-to-heart over Trimming's crash down the stairs at Firenze.

"You can't dogmatise over tumbling downstairs," said Lancing. "If you did an experiment under control and chucked six different people down the same flight of stairs you'd get six different results; one would get off with a few bruises, one would break an arm, one a collar bone, one an ankle, one a femur, one a skull. Broken necks are much rarer, except on stone staircases with awkward corners—but they do happen. And age is a factor; the over-sixty breaks much more easily."

"Quite true," said Dowding, "and if you really got some weight behind it and chucked the over-sixty downstairs with auxiliary velocity, so to speak, the broken neck becomes more like a cert."

"You have a feeling that a little auxiliary power was applied in this case?" asked Lancing, and Dowding nodded.

"Perhaps it's because the vanishing plasterer sticks in my throat. It's not natural," he concluded, "and old Mr. Truby's contribution to the evidence doesn't make it any easier."

"Truby? I haven't heard his bit," said Lancing.

"He seems a very respectable old party—a retired solicitor. He just happened to call in at the Delafield house shortly before the case started," said Dowding, "and he came to us to give a confidential report of an incident that happened while he was there."

Dowding told Lancing about the board which had fallen on Virgilia's head in the drawing-room, and then added: "There are three possible explanations of it. One, accident caused by carelessness (that's Miss Delafield's explanation); two, accident caused by malice aforethought on the part of the plasterer, in which case my guess is that the victim was meant to be Trimming herself; three, accident caused by malice aforethought on the part of Trimming, directed against Miss Delafield."

"But why didn't Miss Delafield report the accident to you herself?" asked Lancing.

"According to Mr. Truby, Miss D. thinks we're making a fuss for the sake of making a fuss," said Dowding. "She said the accident when the board slipped was merely trivial and she saw no sense in making a report about it. You can't blame her, she's had all the upset and worry over her father, and his finances aren't in too good a way—nothing there for anybody as far as I can make out—and she just wants to see the last of us."

"Did Mr. Truby see the plasterer? What's his name, by the way?"

"Name of Walter, according to Miss Delafield. No, Truby didn't see him. Walter was having a cuppa in the kitchen when Truby was there. But several people saw the chap arriving at the house and all the descriptions I can get tally well enough. The postman saw Walter arrive with a handbarrow on the Friday morning, and get his gear out—ladders and boards and so forth. The postman says he was a grey-headed chap with a vacant sort of face. Miss Delafield says the same—she said he looked M.D. And a neighbour says he saw Walter leaving after tea on Tuesday; he loaded his gear up into the barrow and pushed off. Beyond that, no one can tell us anything helpful." Dowding broke off and then added: "It seems a bit rum to me. What's your view—off the record?"

Lancing pondered for a moment; he was being asked for his opinion man to man, not by the powers that be.

"Well, I'd say in a case like this one that there's so much that's rum in the décor, if you take me, that one's got to be damn' careful not to assume that there are abnormalities throughout. Deceased seems to have been a fantastic sort of dame, but that sort can break their necks as easily as the commonplace. The only thing that makes you suspicious is that you can't find the workman who did the ceiling. Assuming this Walter is a nervous dithery old cuss, if he heard his ceiling had collapsed and that people are saying it was his fault that Trimming broke her neck and old Delafield had a stroke, and that he (Walter) had probably robbed the house anyway, perhaps it's not un-natural he's lying low and saying nuffin'. And I gather from what you told me that Miss Delafield thought her father might have employed an old tradesman who had retired—well, it's possible none of his neighbours knew he'd been doing the job and so no report's come in."

Dowding nodded and Lancing looked at him keenly.

"Anything else, mate? I know I've been on some jobs when I'd got nothing to go on but a smell—a sort of sense of uneasiness. Anything of that kind?"

"Nothing I'd put in a report," said Dowding; "but there's this. So far as I can make out, there haven't been any visitors admitted to that house for donkey's years—barring the doctor and some sort of minister of religion. Then this old Truby pays a social call, complete with his niece (a pukka lovely, I'm told), with Roy and with the niece's boy-friend, who butted in later. And it was then that things started happening. It was while the visitors were there the board fell on Miss Delafield's head. And a week or so later, the Trimming does her crash. Added to this, old Truby (who seems the most respectable old bird) seems to have got an idea in his head that Adrian Delafield was very wealthy—which he isn't—and that the house was worth robbing."

"And so?" asked Lancing.

"The only other thing I've got is that the boy-friend, who owns a Lee Jaegar and knows how to drive it, has been seen around the neighbourhood since things started happening. No reason why he shouldn't, of course."

"Know anything about him?" asked Lancing.

"A bit, and I don't want to put a foot wrong. He's in the F.O., and his father's in the British Embassy at Segovia. But Lee Jaegars cost a lot." Dowding came to a determined stop, and after a moment's thought he added: "I could work out a lovely mix up—to amuse myself. And I might add that I think it's quite likely the whole case will be bunged over to you chaps for further consideration. That's my own opinion—nothing else. We've got to a standstill ourselves. We're going to accept an accidental death verdict, but that won't cramp your style if you decide there's anything in it."

"Well, well. I only hope you're right," said Lancing. "Rivers is panting to see that studio."

"He can have it, so far as I'm concerned," said Dowding. "I can't think how the old girl has had the courage to stay there. The eyes in those pictures follow you round. I'd have had 'em all face to the wall before I slept in the place. Fancy waking up and seeing them watching you. Her name's Virgilia, by the way, and she's very high hat. It'll just suit Rivers."

"Virgilia," murmured Lancing. "'My gracious silence...' See *Coriolanus*."

"This one isn't silent. She's very much to the point and says exactly what she thinks," said Dowding.

"Wasn't there a nephew in it somewhere?" asked Lancing, who was very keen to collect all available information against future contingencies.

"Yes. Delafield's grandson, name of Roy Braithwaite. He's a courier, in the tourist racket, but as he was in the south of France at zero hour he's not much use to us."

"Well, it's a beautiful set-up," said Lancing. "Thanks a lot for priming me with the low-down. If anything comes of it,

I'll see you get a commendation for zeal, intelligence and discretion."

"Thanks a lot. I'll swear there's something phoney there, Lancing; but it's more up your street than ours."

2

"It's another of these cases in which you could put forward one solution after another," said Rivers meditatively. "The evidence suggests some lovely variants."

The Divisional police had passed on the Trimming case to the C.I.D. at the Central Office; the full report was now in Rivers's hands—and a very full report it was. The D Division detectives were of the opinion that Trimming's death had been accidental. There was no sign at all of any "breaking and entering," no sign of burglary or larceny and no evidence that any unauthorised person had been on the premises. The one suspicious factor was the missing plasterer.

"The trouble with this case is that there's nobody to answer questions about the normal day-to-day running of the house," said Rivers. "Miss Delafield has been in residence in the studio for nine months, but her motto was 'no interference.' Dr. Mareston died a few days after Trimming died. Dr. Longaby had only been in the house three times. Roy Braithwaite saw his grandfather three times in six months and was quite unobservant of domestic details. Old Delafield himself suffered from failing eyesight and never used a pen for anything but the writing of his weekly cheques, so there are virtually no records. All that Dowding could discover about repairs done to the house was that the exterior was painted seven years ago by a small firm in Paddington which has since gone out of business. The roof was repaired in 1946. Since

1948 no repair work seems to have been done until the drawing-room ceiling was attended to three weeks ago."

"Well, if the old man's total income was £500 a year, there's nothing to be surprised at in that," said Lancing. "But I doubt if there's a house in London into which fewer people have penetrated in ten years."

Rivers nodded. "True enough—Trimming saw to that. It may be worth bearing in mind. Now let's get down to things and choose our own basis. If we're investigating a crime at all, the crime is murder and it's Trimming who was murdered. Why should anybody murder Trimming?"

Lancing was used to the question and answer game; he and Rivers often played it and found it profitable.

"I postulate profit as the motive in this case," replied Lancing. "Contrary to general belief, there was something valuable in that house. X stole it, and X had to kill Trimming because Trimming could have reported that the valuables were missing."

"All right. That's a starting point," said Rivers. "If you're right, it leads to the assumption that Trimming knew about the valuables and old Delafield didn't. It would have been very easy to kill old Delafield, but he wasn't killed. He crawled downstairs and stuck because his heart petered out; and he lay there with his body at an acute angle and his head hanging down and he had a cerebral thrombosis. There's not a bruise on him. So kindly note—he was not killed. He was just left, with the odd chance that he'd be able to talk when he was found."

"Yes, that's quite a point," agreed Lancing. "From which we can argue that old Delafield couldn't tell us anything essential even if he were able to talk. He could only say, 'I heard her fall downstairs' or 'I heard a crash down below and then Trimming screamed, and I heard her fall with the tray.' Evidence of accidental death again; and it'd have taken quite a time for the old boy to have clambered out of bed and crawled on to the landing to see what happened. And while we're talking about seeing, it's worth remembering that that silly gas jet didn't really give enough light for anybody to see anything."

"Trimming kept the gas bill down to two quid a quarter including the cooking," observed Rivers. "Did she get a rake-off on what she saved? There's no evidence of her having been paid a regular salary."

"Here a little and there a little," suggested Lancing. "Had Trimming been doing a savings campaign for quarter of a century? A quid a week saved for twenty-five years and hidden under a floor board in cash? What do you make it? Over a thousand pounds, isn't it? And I've known a lot of people batted over the head for much less than that."

"It's an idea," said Rivers. "It fits in with the theory that old Delafield didn't know anything about a hidden source of valuables. Perhaps the idea was that Delafield was to be left alive to tell the tale—how there wasn't anything valuable, and Trimming, God bless her, was penniless—she'd never accept a penny because he couldn't afford to pay her. And she fell downstairs when the ceiling crashed."

"And instead of staying safe in bed to tell the sad story to Virgilia next day, he scrambled out of bed and had a heart attack from all the excitement," said Lancing.

"Well, it's a picturesque possibility," said Rivers. "But having developed out the idea that Trimming did a savings campaign, perhaps with the pious notion of endowing her own variety of Peculiar Persons, how did X know that Trimming had a secret hoard? She wasn't given to being chatty, so far as I can gather."

"Well, if it's guesses you're asking for, I'll always guess with the best," said Lancing cheerfully. "What about the plasterer? We've postulated an old chap who once worked for a firm held in esteem by Delafield—the firm who built the covered way, for example. It was built in 1912, so perhaps our plasterer was the boy who mixed the mortar in 1912. If he was an old friend, Trimming may have got chatty with him."

"Trimming didn't join the establishment until 1920," put in Rivers, but Lancing was not to be put off.

"That doesn't matter. There'd have been plenty of repairs done to the premises in the 1920s, Delafield was still earning big money then. And if our bloke got to know the house well in the long ago, it'd have been easy for him to search for Trimming's savings."

Rivers sat and pondered, obviously boiling up an idea. Then he said: "Without wishing to be profane, it seems plain that Trimming's mania was of the religious kind. She had a marked kink that way. If she confided in anybody, it would almost certainly have been a fellow-devotee, a follower of her own secret sect—only unfortunately no one can tell us anything about her sect."

"I think I know what you're getting at," said Lancing. "The one person who came to the house before Miss Virgilia butted in was the so-called Minister of Religion—Trimming's variety. Now Miss Virgilia told Dowding that this bloke was next to illiterate, meaning he was uneducated in her sense of the word. She used the description 'local preacher,' implying one of those unordained enthusiasts who bear witness at local revival meetings. It's not unknown for such enthusiasts to go off the rails in other directions."

"The sum total of our cerebration being that local preacher and plasterer may be synonymous," said Rivers. "It's a beautiful thought, but it won't wash. Miss Virgilia saw the plasterer, and if he'd been the local preacher she'd have spotted him. Still, I think the topic is one I could profitably discuss with her. We ought to find the chap who came and visited old Delafield before his daughter put a stop to his visits."

3

"Well, we've put forward enough suggestions to fill a book," said Rivers, some time later. "Most of them are pretty far-fetched, but all of them have a basis in the evidence, inasmuch as they were suggested by some detail in the evidence. Before we go any further, what about answering Miss Virgilia's question. 'If there were a burglar, how did the burglar get out of the house, leaving all the doors and windows fastened behind him?'"

"There's more than one answer to that," said Lancing, "and the classic one is that the burglar didn't get out of the house until he was let out. Having seen to it that everything was bolted, chained and latched, he just waited patiently. It would have been quite easy," he added. "After Longaby smashed in the drawing-room window, he and Miss Virgilia dashed across to the hall and found poor Trimming. After that they both went upstairs, and the drawing-room window stood open. There's a smaller room opening out of the drawing-room. X could have been concealed in there. He'd have had plenty of time to think out methods of getting across six feet of floorboard close by the wainscot without leaving footprints in the dust. And those roads round the Delafield house are so quiet that it's probable X would never have been noticed leaving the house."

"Longaby ought to have got a bobby to help him before he broke in," said Rivers; "but one can't expect everything and the damned house hasn't even got a telephone. I agree with you that

X could have got out as you suggest, but he'd have needed good nerves. It meant waiting for over twelve hours—and it might well have proved to be longer. If he did wait, I should think he's won a record for patience among murderers. Well, as the walrus said, we've had a pleasant chat. The next thing is to decide priorities. I think an intensive search of premises comes first. I know the divisional chaps have searched once, and I'm not suggesting they're not thorough, but an intensive search of a house that size is the hell of a job."

Lancing nodded. "It is and all, but there may be odd documents in odd places—although I have a feeling that Trimming was one of those tidy cusses who loved tidying things up and destroying the bits and pieces which old codgers cherish. She's had a free hand for donkey's years. The old boy's virtually lived in his bedroom for ten years, apart from toddling downstairs very occasionally, and then always with Trimming's assistance. Then there's the studio," he concluded.

"I'm looking forward to that," grinned Rivers. "It should be quite an experience—almost nostalgic. I can remember reproductions of Adrian Delafield's pictures in the Christmas numbers of my youth. We had a 'Hark the herald angels sing' of his in the breakfast-room; my mother doted on it—chubby choir boys."

"Cripes!" said Lancing. "Fancy being brought up in a house with a breakfast-room. I was born in a flat. You ought to enjoy the Delafield house—it'll take you back."

"And talking about being 'taken back,' I have a feeling it'd be worth while trying to find out a bit about Delafield's Paris period," said Rivers. "Henry Fearon would love to do it. He talks French and he knows Paris and its environs, and he might dig up something."

"It's nice to know the case will be popular with somebody," said Lancing. "If he needs a secretary, remember me."

"Not a hope," said Rivers. "You'll probably have to comb the drearier byways of Balham and Tooting seeking a plasterer with a face like a moron. For myself, I propose to start with Mr. Jocelyn Truby. I was rather taken with Dowding's remark to you that the fun and games seemed to originate with the visit of Truby and his young friends. And you might try to contact the niece, and find out if the *fons et origo* of this interest in old Delafield was as simple as appears."

"O.K.," said Lancing. "And I should like to get a line on the boy-friend with the Lee Jaegar. You might leave the method of approach to me. I've never landed you in awkward apologies yet."

"Agreed, but don't fall foul of the F.O. They have a tendency to expect privileged treatment for their superior young sprigs." He stretched his long limbs, and added: "Trimming seems to have roused some repercussions, doesn't she. I think I shall pay a private call on Truby, not taking a witness. He sounds the sort of old boy who might get chattier that way. But you can come with me when I call on Miss Virgilia. You have a knack with elderly ladies, and according to Dowding she can be pretty terse. She's tired of the whole inquiry, and she'll be tireder when she realises we're starting again from the word go."

"It's a bit hard on her," said Lancing. "Dowding says she's involved in writing some scholarly treatise which is held up because she needs to study original documents, and the documents are in the B.M., and the Record Office and the Bodleian, to say nothing of the Sorbonne and other seats of continental learning, and instead of pursuing her original documents she has to be on hand to answer questions put by policemen. Added to which, she doesn't know where the money's coming from to pay the rates, because the old man's annuity isn't enough to pay for his private cubicle."

"She can invite the bailiffs in and let them distrain on the pictures for a start," said Rivers; "but not until I've seen them in situ. The Rating Officer can wait until we've finished. After that he can hold a Dutch auction if he likes, and you can go and bid."

VIII

I

"I'M VERY GLAD TO HEAR IT, CHIEF INSPECTOR," DECLARED Jocelyn Truby; "very glad indeed. I feel most strongly that further investigation is desirable."

Rivers was sitting in Mr. Truby's comfortable old-fashioned sitting-room. It was a room on the first floor of a large house near Portman Square and its long windows gave a pleasant glimpse of the budding plane trees in the square. Truby, Rivers had ascertained, was a widower; he had retired from his profession and given up his big house in Kensington after his wife's death a year ago, and now he was comfortably ensconced with his own furniture in "gentlemen's chambers," in a house run by an elderly married couple who knew what they meant by "gentlemen," and whose competence in the domestic arts ensured that they could pick and choose their tenants.

"I'm very much interested to hear you say that, sir," said Rivers. "I wish you would tell me what causes you to feel strongly about the matter."

Mr. Truby offered Rivers a cigar. Though he was not a cigarette smoker, Mr. Truby enjoyed a good cigar in the evening, and so did Rivers.

"In the course of my legal career, I have occasionally had the feeling that I was up against hocus-pocus," said Truby. "You, as a detective, must know what I mean. The feeling may have no evidence to justify it in the first instance, but I have generally found that evidence was forthcoming when I had the feeling. And several times I have felt suspicious when representing the interests of some person whose lack of acumen, in the legal sense, amounted to a simplicity almost tantamount to stupidity." Truby inhaled his cigar with satisfaction before continuing: "Now I must make it clear that I do not represent Miss Delafield, but I feel a regard for her. Yet, I must admit that I consider her markedly lacking in acumen in the world of affairs. She is a scholar, and her mind is so far removed from mundane considerations that she seems incapable of applying it to such. She tells me, quite simply and without resentment, that her father's means consist only of his annuity and she seems quite content to leave it at that, despite the fact that she herself is very far from affluent."

Truby paused here, and Rivers felt that a question was indicated. "Have you any reason to suppose that Mr. Delafield should possess means beyond his annuity, sir?"

"Well, if he doesn't, I don't know how he got rid of his money," said Truby. "Now I must impress on you that I am basing my impressions on memory, Chief Inspector. I have no material evidence to offer, though you may be able to make good the deficiency. In 1926, if my memory serves me aright, Adrian Delafield was one of the winners in the Spanish American State Lottery. His winnings amounted to a considerable sum—nearly £100,000, if I remember aright. Now 1926 is a long time ago, but consider how Delafield has lived since that date. He lived either in his London house, managed by Trimming, or in his villa at Passy. He has been a man of quiet tastes. I may mention that I met him at one time, on the occasion of commissioning a picture he painted for my old regiment. Admittedly, that is also a very long time ago, but I remember we had some conversation on the subject of finance, his fee being very high. He was then a man of about fifty years, and I remember him saying that a painter has to earn money while his powers are at their height, and to save that money, for in his old age his earning powers will fail." Again Truby paused, and then added: "In my judgment, a man's character does not alter greatly after the age of fifty. Delafield was then a sensible, businesslike fellow, earning a large income and putting some of it by. It seems highly improbable to me that he squandered his capital, so that his income was reduced to £500 a year on the fairly high yield of an annuity."

"That is all very interesting, sir," said Rivers, "and it may be of first-rate importance. You say that you are relying on memory in the matter of the lottery. Can you tell me anything further about it?"

"Only that I took my wife for a cruise in 1926. We went to Buenos Aires, and it was while I was there that the result of the lottery was declared. I was exceedingly interested to learn that one of the winners was Adrian Delafield—a painter whom I had actually met. By the time I returned home, there was enough trouble in this country to make me forget all about lottery winners in South America, but the matter recurred to my mind as soon as I heard Adrian Delafield's name again." Mr. Truby looked at Rivers thoughtfully. "You have the advantage of me by many years, Chief Inspector, but you should be old enough to remember what happened in England in the spring of 1926."

Rivers laughed. "I remember 1926 very well, sir. It occasioned a lot of work for the police—the General Strike."

"Precisely," said Mr. Truby, "and during the General Strike there were no newspapers published—only the official news sheet which was edited, if I remember aright, by Mr. Winston

Churchill. The names of South American lottery winners were not printed in that publication. That is the main reason why Adrian Delafield's good fortune did not become generally known in this country."

"Have you mentioned the subject to Miss Delafield?" inquired Rivers, and Truby replied:

"I have indeed. I gave some thought to the matter. I did not wish to appear as though I were intruding on her affairs, but I felt that I ought to mention it. She denied all knowledge of it. Indeed, I fear she may have thought I was romancing; but when I insisted that I was sure of my facts, she replied characteristically that if her father had been foolish enough to buy lottery tickets, it was quite conceivable that he had been foolish enough to squander the proceeds in other forms of gambling."

2

"The situation gives rise to the wildest conjectures," said Mr. Truby. He was now sipping a modest whisky and soda, and Rivers had accepted a similar drink. "One always comes back to Trimming," went on Mr. Truby.

Rivers nodded. "Yes. I shall always regret that I never saw her. What opinion did you form of Trimming, Mr. Truby?"

"I think she was a dangerous woman," replied Jocelyn. "I do not wish to use the word 'mad' unadvisedly. I accept that Trimming was not mad in the sense of being certifiable, but she was certainly peculiar and eccentric to a marked degree. She was also a dominating possessive woman. Now consider Delafield's history from the outbreak of war in 1939. He remained in France, with Trimming ordering his household. I do not know if you deprecate conjectures, Chief Inspector?"

"Far from it. Conjecture has to form the basis of detection when facts are missing," said Rivers cheerfully. "I hope you will conjecture freely, Mr. Truby."

"Excellent," beamed the old solicitor. "Now I would hazard as a reasonable possibility that Adrian Delafield had invested his winnings in France. He spent more and more time in France, and it is notorious that at that date tax evasion was much easier in France than in England, and even basic taxation was much lower than in England. Delafield stayed in France until the country surrendered to the Germans, and then, by what route and what methods is unknown, Trimming got him to the coast and they eventually arrived in England, with a group of other refugees, in a fishing boat. Delafield was then a very sick man, quite incapable of making decisions for himself. It is interesting to conjecture what happened to any capital he had in France."

"Very interesting," said Rivers. "We shall go into all that with the French authorities; they have records of all property seized by the Germans—if that is what you are thinking about."

"I'm not thinking of anything so rational," said Truby cheerfully. "I'm wondering what Trimming got away with, or what Trimming managed to hide. I told you my line was conjecture."

"And a very interesting conjecture, too," agreed Rivers; "but the thing which interests me is this. How much of this famous escape story can be regarded as objective fact, and how much is hearsay?"

"Bless you, it's all hearsay," said Truby. "Trimming talked to Dr. Mareston and Dr. Mareston talked to other people. Old Delafield talked to Mareston—but Mareston is dead. How much objective fact you will be able to sort out I do not know. I suppose it depends on how many official records remain. But one thing seems pretty certain. Trimming reappeared in St. John's Wood in the autumn of 1940 with a very shaky and enfeebled old dodderer in her charge. She had the keys of Firenze and she must have notified the local police of their return, and got the necessary identity cards and other documents for herself and her employer." Truby chuckled. "I think it's a very good thing the case has been passed to your department, Chief Inspector. It's going to take a lot of work to sort it all out."

3

"The picture, as you see it, is Trimming in control all round, Mr. Truby," said Rivers. "Now you saw Mr. Delafield. What did you make of him?"

"He was remarkably spry," said Truby. "He remembered me—or said he remembered me. He also remembered the names of my fellow-officers in the picture he painted; but as the names were entered on the cartoon, there's nothing much in that. But he wasn't senile. He was perfectly *compos mentis,* and if he had wanted to complain of Trimming to Dr. Longaby, he could have done so. He obviously didn't want to. Trimming kept him very comfortable and he was quite satisfied with things as they were, barring a few grumbles natural to advanced age. I like your phrase—Trimming was in control. She'd got things as she wanted them, except for the presence in the studio of Miss Delafield. That's my opinion. Trimming wanted to get rid of Miss Virgilia by hook or by crook. All the nonsense she talked to me about 'evil in the house' was directed against Miss Virgilia. If Trimming had mistrusted the chap who was working in the drawing-room, she'd got the remedy in her own hands—she could have refused to admit him. Far more likely, to my mind, that Trimming got the plasterer in to help her in some little idea of her own."

"It's an interesting theory," said Rivers, and Jocelyn Truby cocked an intelligent eye at him.

"Not got on the trace of the plasterer yet?"

"Not yet," said Rivers.

"Makes you wonder if he is a plasterer," said Truby. "Anyway, I've no doubt he was an ally of Trimming's."

"Helping Trimming to make a hidey-hole for her savings and salvagings," suggested Rivers. "If that was it, I don't wonder Trimming was startled when she heard the ceiling come down. Hiding things in the plaster of the ceiling is a new one on me."

Truby chuckled. "Or perhaps the ceiling was a blind," he suggested. "But my idea fits in more ways than one. It was Miss Virgilia who insisted that the ceiling must be repaired."

"And put ideas into Trimming's head," said Rivers. "A hidey-hole for herself and a knock on the head for Miss Virgilia. But if that was it, I'm surprised that she organised the booby-trap on the one day when visitors were coming to the house; or perhaps she didn't know the visitors were coming."

"But she did!" exclaimed Mr. Truby, with animation. "Trimming knew I was coming—she was all prepared. And I beg to differ from you concerning the improbability of organising an accident when visitors were expected. The visitors were a safeguard. If Miss Virgilia had been badly hurt when there was nobody in the house save Trimming herself, the incident would have looked much more suspicious. In my judgment, the accident was very well timed—but not very well organised, seeing it miscarried." Mr. Truby looked at Rivers almost roguishly; the old man was enjoying himself. "I told you that this sequence of events roused the wildest conjectures in my mind," he went on. "Could there be a possibility that Trimming, having failed once, arranged a second booby-trap in order to get rid of Miss Virgilia? That the drugget and stair rod was so arranged that whoever came downstairs was certain to fall over it; but Trimming was so startled by the collapse of the ceiling that she forgot her own trap and tripped over it herself?"

Rivers laughed. "Like the malefactor in the book of Psalms who dug a pit privily and fell into the midst of it himself. It's an ingenious idea, sir, but it doesn't carry conviction. I prefer the idea of the absconding plasterer myself."

"Well, perhaps... Dear me. Come in."

4

A second visitor had come to call on Mr. Truby, and Rivers felt that his luck was in. The fair sunburned fellow who came into the room was announced as Mr. Braithwaite by the lugubrious looking butler-valet-landlord who attended to Mr. Truby's needs. Rivers was well briefed in the personnel of his case, and he knew this young man to be Adrian Delafield's grandson and Miss Virgilia's nephew, Roy. Mr. Truby had no intentions of being cagey about the presence of Scotland Yard in his sitting-room. He greeted Roy cheerfully, adding: "It's very fortunate that you should have happened to call, young man. This is Chief Inspector Rivers, C.I.D., who has taken over the investigation into Trimming's death."

Roy said: "Cripes!" Rivers heard it quite clearly, but it was followed by a cheerful grin as Truby completed the introduction.

"Good evening," said the young man. "Sorry if I dropped my bundle a bit, but I hadn't realised that Trimming had attained Yard status. Was she murdered?" he inquired in conclusion.

"I don't know. But I'm hoping to find out," replied Rivers.

Delafield's grandson had nothing of the aesthete about him, Rivers noticed. He was of middle height, with good broad shoulders, and he held himself well. He wore a pleasant tweed jacket—greenish-blue—grey flannel slacks and a clean shirt and collar. His fair hair was well brushed, and his face tanned by a sun which had been hotter than an April sun in England.

"What's your opinion on the matter, Mr. Braithwaite?" asked Rivers, alert, as always, for a first impression.

"Well, I won't pretend I haven't chewed over the pros and cons," said Roy. "When my aunt told me about the inquest being adjourned, I supposed the cops had found something we don't know about. But why murder Trimming? I know she was a maddening old funny, but she's been that for donkey's years and nobody took direct action. However, I suppose you know all the answers and we don't."

"I certainly don't," said Rivers, and Roy shrugged his shoulders.

"As you say. But what I came to talk to Mr. Truby about wasn't Trimming at all." He turned to Jocelyn. "The law of inheritance isn't my long suit, sir. I've come to cadge information." He grinned—a pleasant deprecating grin. "Auntie V. told me how kind you'd been and I thought you might include me. You see the frightful thing—the really frightful thing—is that the old boy hasn't made a will, or if he has no one can find it, and it looks as though the fag end of that ghastly lease may fall in on me and Auntie V. And Auntie V.'s been talking about dilapidations." He turned to Rivers. "You see the point? Whoever is the owner of the lease when it peters out has to meet the ground landlord's extortions. And that house will swallow up a fortune."

"Yes. I see the point. But aren't you meeting trouble half-way?" said Rivers. "Your grandfather may live for two years. I've known several patients in his condition last a surprisingly long time."

"Well, the doctors don't seem to think so," said Roy gloomily. "I don't care a blue hoot about dilapidations myself. I can easily beat it..." He broke off and his endearing grin flashed out. "Is declining to inherit the fag end of a lease an extraditable offence, sir?"

"If you're asking me, I require notice of that question. But I should say not," said Rivers. "The ground landlord can distrain on deceased's property, but that's about as far as he's likely to go, I imagine."

"He's welcome," said Roy. "He can have the pictures." He turned back to Jocelyn Truby. "It's Auntie V. I'm worrying about. I don't see why she should be bothered by it all. She was pretty noble, coming and butting in to see that the old boy wasn't bullied into his grave by Trimming praying over him, and I don't think it ever entered her head to bother about what happened to his property when he packed up. She just assumed he'd leave it all to Trimming, if there was anything to leave, and Auntie V. was very fair over it and said Trimming had earned it. And now Trimming's gone and done the dirty on us. It really is a mess up."

"Did you see much of Trimming, Mr. Braithwaite?" inquired Rivers.

"Depends what you call much," replied Roy. "I can remember her as long as I can remember anything, because I used to be taken to see the old man when my mother was alive. There was a gap during the war and after, of course. I went into the army straight from school, and after the war I went to Neuchâtel and read modern languages, and I wasn't in England at all until 1949. Then—oh, I just didn't bother. One doesn't, these days. It wasn't till Auntie V. settled in the studio that I saw the old boy again. I suppose I've been along there about half a dozen times in the last six months, but more to see the aunt than the old man."

"Did he remember you?" asked Mr. Truby, and Rivers was interested in his putting this question.

"Well, I think it would be expecting rather a lot of him to recognise me, if that's what you mean," said Roy. "He'd seen me last in 1938, when I was eleven. He remembered my existence all right, because he'd painted me when I was six. Auntie V. took me into his room, and said, 'This is Roy,' and the Ancient said, 'How you've grown,' or the equivalent, and asked if I'd still got the portrait—which shows his memory was a bit blah, because he knew my mother's house was bombed. But he was quite affable and accepted me, so to speak."

"Did you remember him?" persisted Jocelyn Truby.

"More or less—in the way that kids do remember the aged," replied Roy patiently. "I remembered his beard—very natty and artistic, and his white hair. He's still got a good crop of hair considering his age; when I saw him before it was what might be called luxuriant. But I remembered Trimming much better; she used to make me doughnuts for tea and meringues to follow. She made doughnuts again when I went to see the Ancient last March." He paused, and turned to Rivers. "I suppose it's out of order to ask you questions, Chief Inspector. But are you really brooding over the notion that Trimming was murdered? Auntie V. was always saying that Trimming was mad, and up to a point I suppose she was, but it seems even madder to me to suppose somebody murdered her. Why? I don't see what they got out of it."

"Sorry, I can't answer that one, because I don't know, any more than you do," said Rivers. "The thing which has really given rise to suspicion is that the plasterer can't be traced."

"Lord, he couldn't have murdered Trimming," said Roy. "She was pretty old, but she was still a fairly hefty female. My aunt says the plasterer was a dithery old customer, really old, and too frightened to say a word to anybody. Trimming could have chucked him downstairs much more easily than he could have chucked her. If you'd seen Trimming shaking mats and whanging carpets as I have, you'd know what I mean. Still, I suppose it's no use arguing."

He turned back to Mr. Truby.

"I'm sorry I butted in, sir, but if you could give the aunt a word of advice about this lease business, I know she'd be grateful. She's honestly worried stiff. It's bad enough for her having all this to-do about Trimming, without having to worry about ruinous inheritances."

"Yes, yes. I'll have a word with Miss Delafield about the matter," replied Truby. "I agree with the Chief Inspector—it's premature to worry about it now, but she must take advice when we see how things go."

"Thanks a lot, sir, and good-bye for now."

He turned to Rivers. "Does it mean you're starting the whole inquisition all over again?"

"I'm afraid so. We shan't need to go over the evidence already established, but the inquiry will be wider in scope. I shall be very glad of your help in certain respects, Mr. Braithwaite. Will you be available for the next few days?"

"I haven't got another job on till next week, so I can meet you any time you like. Incidentally, I should like to get my aunt out of that damned studio. She's all by herself and with the house empty I don't much like it."

"There's no reason why Miss Delafield shouldn't make other arrangements," said Rivers, "though I don't think you need be apprehensive of her safety."

"It's not that so much," rejoined Roy; "but it must be hideously depressing for her. She feels she made a mucker about looking after her father, and with the police force indicating that Trimming was murdered just across the way it's not too cheerful, and the press hounds will be buzzing around like the hosts of Midian as soon as they know your lot's on the go. However, life's like that. When do you want me to appear?"

"To-morrow morning if you can manage it," replied Rivers. "Say ten-thirty, at the house."

"At Firenze. Don't I wish I were there… Right. I'll be along, but don't expect too much. I don't know much about the Ancient, and even less about Trimming."

5

After Roy had gone, Jocelyn Truby turned to Rivers with a twinkle in his eye.

"Did my wildest conjecture convey itself to you, Chief Inspector?"

"I rather think it did," said Rivers, "and if I'm right, your idea is certainly a tall one. Are you asking yourself what incontrovertible proof there is that the aged gentleman tended by Trimming was in fact Adrian Delafield?"

"Well, what proof is there?" demanded the irrepressible Truby. "His daughter's testimony? She had barely seen him for over a quarter of a century. His grandson's? The recollection of a boy of eleven. My own? I hadn't seen him since 1920, and the room was too dark to see him anyway."

"And when did the hypothetical change over occur?" demanded Rivers.

"Why, when Trimming brought him back from France. He was a valuable property."

Truby began to laugh. "Fantastic or not, wild conjecture or not, there's still a chance it's a fact," he chuckled. "And how, Chief Inspector, can you ever prove it, one way or the other?"

"On the spur of the moment I can't tell you," rejoined Rivers. "I shall have to think it out."

IX

1

"Well, it's a new one on me," said Roy. "My mother couldn't have known anything about it, or she'd have told us. And Auntie V. never heard about it either. Do you think old Truby's got mixed up? It's a long time ago."

Such was Roy Braithwaite's reaction when Rivers mentioned the Spanish American Lottery said to have been won by Adrian Delafield in the year 1926.

"It doesn't seem such a long time to Mr. Truby as it does to you," said Rivers, and Roy grinned.

"Probably not—he's always rubbing it in; time is relative. May, 1926. I wasn't born till a month later. We were living at Ospedalletti—not far from Ventimille. D'you mind if I beat through the family history and see if I can sort things out?"

"I should be very glad if you would," said Rivers. "You're my best hope of getting Mr. Delafield's past life described."

"Don't be too jolly hopeful. I know mighty little about him—except that he was a stingy old blighter. Family histories are generally on the squalid side, and ours is no exception," said Roy. "You know he kicked Auntie V. out, just because she was determined to go to Cambridge? Well, he created when my mother got married: he and my father hated one another like stink. But that's all by the way. 1926—Ospedalletti. The pater was on sick leave—he was in the Consular Service—he had rotten health, and they went into Italy because it was cheaper than France. Of course I can't remember anything about it, but I've been back there since, just out of curiosity to see where I was born. It was a rather mangy villa up in the hills. Come to think of it, unless the Ancient told her, my mother wouldn't have heard anything about his windfall. It wasn't the sort of place where you got papers, and wireless hadn't got going then, had it?"

"Wireless sets weren't very common, and what is called 'coverage' wasn't complete," said Rivers. "Did you ever hear where your grandfather was living in 1926?"

"Here, wasn't he? Or wait a jiff. He got the villa in Passy round about that time or a bit later. I heard something about that when I was older, because Adrian—my brother—was ten in 1926, and mother wanted to send him to school in England and couldn't afford it, and she wanted to ask the Ancient to cough up funds to help, and Father wouldn't let her. Father got back to a job in 1927, in Lucerne. We were there till he died, in 1931. Lucerne is the first place I can remember." He paused, sitting thinking with wrinkled brows. "I told you it was all pretty squalid," he went on. "My parents were often broke, because of Father being ill, and there were always arguments about whether to ask the Ancient for help I don't believe he ever did help. Probably Trimming squashed it—she'd got him just there."

Roy put his thumb down and continued: "In 1932 we came back to London, mother and Adrian and me. That was when he painted my portrait. He called it 'Heaven lies about us in our infancy'—fact. It was exhibited. But fortunately nobody remembers it."

"Was that portrait painted here?" asked Rivers.

"Yes, in the studio—and Trimming fed me doughnuts and meringues. I think the Ancient may have produced some funds that time, because Adrian stayed at school in England, and Mother and I went to live in Grenoble. She'd got friends there." He broke off, and said: "Look here, am I just wasting your time? I don't seem to be getting anywhere."

"Don't worry about that," said Rivers. "I'm getting a background, which is what I need. We've got up to 1932, when you were six. Your father had died and your mother had two sons to educate and was hard put to it. Do you ever remember your mother saying that your grandfather was very wealthy?"

"Yes, of course she did. It was the *leitmotif* of our youth, 'Father could help so easily. He gets enormous prices for his pictures'—but never a suggestion that he'd walloped up the winnings on a lottery. I still think that's a make-up—or mix-up—of old Truby's. The wish fathering the thought, perhaps."

Rivers twitched an eyebrow inquiringly. "Meaning?"

"Oh, nothing, really. But he seems to be developing a thing about Auntie V. But getting back to the long ago. It was when we were in Grenoble that mother started writing—and got away with it. She wrote novels under the name of Rosamund Casterton. I never read any of them, and I believe they were pretty sick-making, but she made a lot of money—a lot for those days, anyway. She educated me out of them, and sent Adrian to Oxford. Rather marvellous, you know. I often think of her, pouring out heart throbs with her tongue in her cheek, just to get us educated. Though it did mean a decent time for her as well—nice clothes and nice food and living where she liked." He halted and sat staring out of the window for a moment as though his thoughts were far away, and then added, as though speaking to himself: "Women do that sort of thing more easily than men, most men, anyway. Mrs. Trollope did it—Anthony's mother—and there were people like Elinor Glynn and Maud Diver… Sorry, I'm woolgathering. Where were we?"

"In the middle nineteen thirties, when you were ten. Did you go on living in France?"

"Mother did, until 1936. I went to prep. school in England in 1935, and in '36 Mother took a house in Chelsea. Rather a nice small house. It was bombed in 1940—and she was in it. Direct hit."

"Do you remember if she came here to see your grandfather?"

"Yes, sometimes. I know she talked about Trimming. But the old man spent more and more time in France. I believe he was a wicked old scallywag. Perhaps that's how he spent his winnings—if he ever scooped them."

"Did you ever see his house in Passy?"

"No. I went there once, meaning to have a look at it, after the war—in 1947. But it didn't exist. It'd been burnt down. I believe some collaborators lived there during the German occupation, and the resistance boys burnt it in 1945." He stopped abruptly and looked at Rivers with amused inquiring eyes. "What the heck has all this got to do with Trimming falling downstairs?" he asked.

2

"It's a perfectly fair question," said Rivers reasonably. (He was a very reasonable, considerate investigator.) "The point at issue is: Did anybody kill Trimming? I've got to regard it as an open question. But if somebody did kill her, they did it for a reason—a motive. And the most probable motive is profit."

"O.K.," said Roy cheerfully. "I see what you're getting at. Trimming snaffled the Ancient's winnings—what was left of them. How? Do you think she just stole, embezzled or what have you? Or got it by undue influence, as the saying is?"

"If anything of the kind happened, my guess would be that she managed to bring easily portable valuables into this country when she arrived as a refugee with your grandfather, in 1940," said Rivers, and Roy sat up, looking cheerful.

"That's a beautiful idea. Diamonds lacquered over to look like beads or studs or boot buttons, or variations on that theme. And she hid them somewhere in this house and gloated over them in secret; like a miser. But why on earth did she tell anybody about it, or show them where the loot was hidden? I think the story breaks down there. Trimming never told anybody anything. She was an awfully secret person. And if she'd got all this wealth, why the heck did she go on living as a domestic and slave to save pennies for the old man? That part sounds a bit bats; but I'm all in favour of finding buried treasure on the premises." He stared at Rivers again, alert and entertained. "It's a wonderful story, but do you really believe it? Isn't it really just story spinning? I know Trimming was fantastic, but I can't see her pinching the old man's valuables. I just don't believe it. She doted on him."

"I think it's true that if a person is abnormal in one way, they may be abnormal in another," said Rivers. "Your aunt says that Trimming was mad; you say she was fantastic. I prefer the word abnormal. But let's leave what you call the story spinning out of it and get back to facts. First, you had never heard that your grandfather won a large prize in a lottery?"

"Never, and that means that neither my father nor Mother had ever heard of it either, because Mother would have told me. I just don't believe it—or I shan't unless you can prove it. Is it provable? Will there be records of the Spanish American Lottery winners in 1926?"

"I don't know," said Rivers; "but that is one of the jobs my department will delve at. The particular organisation which ran that lottery has been liquidated long since, but it may be possible to get information in other ways. Thirty years doesn't seem such a long time to people who're in their sixties, you know."

"Like old Jos Truby," said Roy cheerfully. "I say, you will try to find out, won't you? If you get on the track, there may be a hope for Auntie V. and self. The Ancient may have salted something away in France and forgotten all about it when he had his seizure during the famous escape. Glory! There may be a few million francs sitting unsuspected in the Crédit Lyonnais or somewhere. The French would never cough up funds unless someone progged them."

"It'll be looked into," said Rivers. "We're sending a chap out to Passy to try to trace Mr. Delafield's banking transactions in France."

"Are you really? Cheers!" said Roy. "I'm beginning to believe in the lottery after all, hearing you talk about banking transactions in an official tone of voice."

"Don't be too hopeful," said Rivers dryly. "Now you were talking about the 'famous escape,' meaning when Trimming got Mr. Delafield back from France, I take it. When did you first hear the story?"

"When I was at school. Oh, lord, aren't you a chap for digging! You ought to have been an archæologist. I told you our house was bombed and Mother was killed. I was down in Cornwall; Prinners, my school, was evacuated there. The Head told me about it—he was a decent old bird. I felt a bit—well, flattened out; and then there was all the huroosh about money—school fees and all that. There were still royalties coming in from Mother's books then, and some war damage, and old Heatherington, my headmaster, did his best to tidy it up and stood as guardian or what have you. It was he who told me that my grandfather had got back to England and suggested putting in an application for help until things were tidied up. I was furious—so was Adrian, my brother. He didn't get his till 1941. You see the Ancient had been such a filthy old skinflint when mother really did need help, that neither Adrian nor I wanted to have anything to do with him. In any case, he was quite gaga at the time, so Heatherington gave it best."

Again Roy studied Rivers's face. "You're not trying to destroy the legend, are you? It's grown to quite a legend, with Trimming shoving the old man in a wheelbarrow on the last bit, and pretending to collect whelks or mussels on the rocks until she found a fisherman who could be bribed to chance the trip. It's a glorious story."

"It certainly is," said Rivers. "Did your grandfather tell you about it?"

"No. Trimming told me not to talk to him about it. She said it upset him. But she told me a few bits: how they left Passy in a car and ran out of petrol and took to their feet and trudged to the coast. She meant to try for Dieppe, because it was nearest, and she knew it, but they eventually got off somewhere between Fécamp and Senneville. I don't see why not," he concluded. "Lashings of people did get over in small boats at that time."

Rivers nodded, and Roy demanded: "Why look so sceptical? It's known the Ancient was in Passy before the French packed up, and he arrived here at his own house a month or so later, and it must have been quite a trip."

Again Rivers nodded. "And you did not see him again until your aunt came to live in the studio?"

"That's it. I'd been abroad most of the interim, and I didn't really care if I ever saw the old blighter again, but I'd kept in touch with Auntie V., more or less. She used to write to me from Canada during the war and send me parcels. She's a decent old scout. When she settled here she asked me to come and see the Ancient. She's much kinder-hearted than I am."

"Well, thanks a lot for your patience in answering all my questions," said Rivers. "You've given me a much clearer idea of your grandfather than I had before. And now for a question which you may think ridiculous. Don't be in a hurry to answer it; take your time and think it out. Have you any means of being quite certain that the grandfather you saw again here, after a considerable lapse of years, was in fact identical with the grandfather you saw when you were a schoolboy?"

"Good God!" exclaimed Roy. And then he began to laugh.

3

He laughed for quite a while, and then he said: "It's a wonderful idea. What on earth made you think that one up? Well, as an answer to your question, I just took it for granted. There was Trimming (no mistaken identity about her—she's unmistakable) and the house, and the old boy, and there was no earthly reason why I should imagine he was a different old boy. And he's not, you know. I find it awfully difficult to tell you why I'm sure, but I am sure. There's the way he talked, and the way he moves his hands, and something about him—I can't tell you what—that reminds me of Mother. Besides, there's Auntie V. Are you going to tell me she doesn't know her own father? I should like to be there when you try to put that one across her—she'll be livid. Auntie V.'s quite certain about what she knows and what she doesn't know."

"I shall be seeing your aunt later," said Rivers. "At the moment I'm concentrating on you. You'd be prepared to go into the witness box and swear on oath that the grandfather you saw last about 1938 is the same man you talked to here during the last six months?"

Roy sat very still, no laughter in his eyes now, and it was some time before he answered. Then he said:

"Yes. I should. If asked that question on oath, I should just answer 'Yes. He's the same man. I know he is.'"

"How do you know?"

"That's much more difficult to answer," said Roy slowly. "I think one has a certain awareness about close relations; not intuition, or anything as vague as that, but a recognition of something common to one's own family—an expression on an old face that makes one remember a young face. I've thought of my brother sometimes when I saw the Ancient's nose and chin; and I've seen my mother in the way he moves his hands. I know I can't prove it, but your bright idea is quite wrong. I know it is—and neither judge nor jury nor counsel nor detective will make me say anything else."

"Thanks very much. I'm glad you know your own mind," said Rivers.

"Did you think of that entirely on your own?" asked Roy.

Rivers laughed a little. "It's possible for more than one person to raise identical questions suggested by the evidence," he replied.

Roy nodded. "Yes. I see that. I just wondered if old Truby had been sticking his oar in."

"Why? Did he raise the point with you?"

"Not exactly. But after he'd been here to see the Ancient, we all went off for a drink at his place—Truby and his niece, Susan, and a chap who's a friend of hers whom I happened to know in the army—name of Raven. He brought his car along to give Susan a lift home, and we all bunged in and went to have a sherry with Uncle Truby. And it was then that Raven got asking questions about Trimming and what happened when she brought the old man back here in 1940, and I thought Uncle Truby looked as though he was boiling an idea up. He's like that."

Rivers nodded—and waited; he was getting interested in Roy, who was showing himself a much more thoughtful fellow than he had at first appeared. Roy went on after a moment or two:

"I know the story of Trimming and the way she behaved before Auntie V. butted in does give support to your bright idea. She wouldn't let anybody see the Ancient, and people honestly thought he was dead. People do think things like that, especially if there's an eccentric in charge, like Trimming. But you see people were quite wrong. He wasn't dead—and he isn't dead. She'd slaved to look after him, and he'd been jolly well looked after."

"Yes," said Rivers. "Nobody disputes that. But can you accept it as credible that an old man, even an invalid would be willing to live in complete isolation for year after year, seeing no one but Trimming, unless he had something to conceal."

"Look here," said Roy, sitting up and sounding more restive; "you're arguing that Trimming had done a change-over act with the Ancient, substituting a different old man in place of my grandfather. If she pulled that one off, she was pretty clever—and so was he. She'd have been intelligent enough to see that she'd got to let him be seen—establish him with the neighbours. She'd have asked people in to have a look at him and get used to him. He needn't have talked, or answered questions—too far gone to talk. But she'd never have dared let those rumours get around about his being dead. It'd have been much too near the ham bone if your idea were the right one."

Roy got up and wandered round the room. They were sitting in the dining-room at Firenze, and an old and out-of-date gas fire poppled and hissed unwillingly under its asbestos fuel.

"What a hideous room this is," said Roy. "Funny to think the Ancient was regarded as one of the country's leading artists and his home as an exemplar of fine taste—though lots of artists have damn' queer taste in their own households. Look here, sir." He turned to Rivers with a change in his voice. "You've got this idea, and I know you're wrong. I can't prove it, but I do know it, and Auntie V. will know it even better than I do. You go and talk to her; she'll probably think up something that settles it. Anyway, my grandfather's still alive; he can't talk or tell you who he is, but he's still there to look at. And there must be somebody, apart from old Jos Truby, who knew him before he retired to his bedroom for keeps. If you can't find anybody, I will. It's silly to think there's no one who remembers him."

"Right-o," said Rivers. "You keep on saying I've got this idea. Detectives can't afford to take ideas for granted, but they have to consider them and get them out of the way. And now, before you go, will you let me have your itinerary for the days you were away in France, when Trimming was killed—just to clear you out of the way."

Roy grinned. "O.K. That's an easy one. Here goes."

4

Roy took a diary out of his pocket, saying: "Auntie V. and I got busy putting dates down, because she wanted to get clear about exactly which days the plasterer was working here. He didn't come every day—some blah about the ceiling needing to dry before he did the next bit. That any interest to you?"

"Yes, certainly," said Rivers. "I didn't realise he gave some days a miss."

"Oh, he was one of these slow-going old blighters, took his own time. Now here's a calendar of dates for you—you can check them again with Auntie V. She worked it out and I checked up with the days I knew about. Here goes. She started her calendar with

Monday, 22nd March, because that was the first day Dr. Longaby called to see the Ancient. For some reason Auntie V. feels Longaby is so reliable that it helps her to know exactly when he came—his visits helped to fix the other days in her mind. Walter—the plasterer—brought his gear here on Friday, 26th, but he didn't do any work that day so far as we can make out—just inspected the ceiling, said it was a bigger job than he expected, and dumped his gear. He started working on the Monday, the 29th, and he worked for the three following days. I know he was here on the 29th, because I came to ask Auntie V. if I could bring the Trubys to tea on the Wednesday—the 31st. He was working here that day, but he gave it a miss on the Friday and Saturday. Longaby looked in again on Thursday of that week—1st April."

"Right," said Rivers. "And the Trubys came to tea on the 31st, when the board fell on Miss Delafield."

"That's right. Walter turned up again on Monday 5th, and finished on Tuesday 6th. So much for him. I crossed to France on Saturday, 3rd April. I wasn't due for my job in Avignon until the 6th, but I hitched down through France and pocketed the travelling allowance. On Saturday, the 3rd, I slept in Paris; on Sunday 4th, in Auxerre; on Monday 5th, in Lyons, and on the 6th I arrived in Avignon. Addresses of where I stayed all written out here, if you want them."

"Thanks," said Rivers. "And the names of your clients?"

"Mr. and Mrs. Silas K. Williams of Detroit, U.S.A. Wealthy Yanks, 'doing Europe'—and jolly decent folks, too. They wanted a courier to take them around Avignon, Arles, Nîmes, the Stes Maries and all the rest, so they didn't miss anything. They applied to Universitas—my old firm—and I was offered the job. I left the Williamses—with mutual regrets—on the 10th, after I'd got Auntie V.'s wire about the mess-up here. I gave her an address in

Toulon, so I didn't hear what had happened until I arrived there. My party was working on along the Riviera coast into Italy, and they didn't really need a courier again until they got to Rome—and there are lashings of guides there. Here's the testimonial they wrote me—very handsome, considering I left them high and dry."

While Rivers glanced through the kindly words written by Mr. Silas K. Williams in appreciation of Mr. Roy Braithwaite's erudition, kindliness and efficiency, the Chief Inspector found time to reflect that this seemed a pretty clear alibi (already checked as far as time permitted) for the night of Wednesday, 7th April, when Trimming broke her neck in London, N.W.8. He looked up and caught Roy grinning at him.

"Sorry, Chief," said the young man. "I know it's not really funny, but the whole thing seems crazy to me. Here have I told you my life story and given you the low-down on family squabbles, to say nothing of a lecture on recognising my own grandfather, all because poor dotty old Trimming fell downstairs and put paid to herself through tripping over a stair rod." He paused and stretched his hands out, palms upward. "Do you really believe any of it—the story that Trimming pinched a fortune, hid it for years—and then told Wallie, the plasterer, all about it? Because I do not."

"Believing isn't any part of a detective's job, not without evidence to support the belief," said Rivers. "Detection consists of answering questions. The chief question I want answered is 'Where is Wally, the plasterer?'"

"Lying low in his own bed-sitter, in Kilburn or Paddington or Notting Dale or Lisson Grove—anywhere within push-barrow distance of this house—hoping you won't find him and involve him in the repercussions of his rotten plastering," replied Roy. "It might have been the ceiling falling down that made Trimming trip up, but I can't see it was really Wally's fault, poor old moron."

X

I

"I DO HOPE I'M NOT DISTURBING YOU, MISS DELAFIELD. I JUST wanted to tell you how sorry I am about all the worry you've had."

Susan Truby stood at the front door of the studio with a sheaf of irises in her hands; she was bare-headed, clad in a neat skirt and short-sleeved blue pullover, for it was a warm April evening. Virgilia Delafield, who was far from lacking in artistry, thought that Susan, slender, blue-eyed, black-haired, was as graceful as the flowers she carried.

"My dear child—how kind of you. You're not disturbing me at all. Come in. And are those lovely flowers for me? I'm so fond of irises—'sweet flower de luce'—and I can't tell you how long it is since anybody brought me a bunch of flowers." She glanced over Susan's shoulder and saw Peter Raven's big car and smiled. "Is that your tall friend? Won't he come in too? Roy will be coming presently."

"I'm sure he'd love to," replied Susan, and called to Peter, who slid out of the car and came to shake hands with Miss Delafield.

"If you're quite sure we're not a nuisance we should love to look at the pictures again," he said. "Susan and I have been having an argument about them. The swing of the pendulum, you know—wondering whether the pendulum has swung too far in our generation."

Virgilia gave a little cackle of laughter. "The pictures? My dear young man; I'm afraid even the bailiffs and broker's men wouldn't touch them with a barge pole. But come in, both of you."

They walked into the studio, which looked even more startling than usual in the clear afternoon light, and Susan said:

"It's almost baroque. Or is it rococo the word I want? All these vivid reds and blues and yellows."

"Pure primary colour," said Miss Virgilia, as she went to fetch a vase for the irises. She set them on her desk, and added: "I've got to know my father's work rather dreadfully well since I've lived here. If only the subjects weren't so intrusive, I think there's a modicum of merit in the compositions. You get so tired of recognising the figures and the stories." She stared across at a simpering Joan of Arc, and added: "It may sound absurd, but I've begun to correlate these story-book pictures with Trimming's expression of religion—all pure cliché, with silly phrases like the torments of the damned and the joys of salvation put in as automatically as the fair hair of the angels in father's pictures. Perhaps their minds had something in common."

"But that's jolly interesting," said Peter Raven, who was always quick to recognise an original idea when he met one. "Could one find common ground for both minds in the embellishments of so many Italian churches—the painted plaster madonnas in tinsel frocks and brassy crowns, and the agonies of emaciated saints—the insistence on representation of a sort which the simplest mind can't fail to recognise."

Miss Virgilia looked at him with fresh interest. "That is a very fair analogy," she said, but Susan put in:

"Leaving out all the introspection—you see, I'm not an intro., I'm all extravert—it's the drawing Peter and I were talking about. When I got home after I'd seen all these, it suddenly occurred to me that I can't draw at all. Not like that. None of us can. We do small 'clevers.' If I started on a canvas that size, I should be sunk."

"I'm sure you don't want to start on anything that size, and it'd be terribly expensive," said Miss Virgilia.

Susan laughed a little. "Gosh! Wouldn't it? Materials cost the earth. Was this Mr. Delafield's favourite palette?"

The palette, still adorned with thick blobs of paint, and with brushes stuck through the thumb hole, was in a glass case, surrounded by heavy mouldings, in a corner behind Miss Virgilia's desk. (The latter was a plain deal table but so covered with papers and books that it achieved almost a decorative quality of its own.) The elderly lady gave an impatient snort.

"Favourite palette, indeed. Pure snobbery, my dear. It was after he painted Alexandra. The portrait was commissioned by some nursing association and he went to Marlborough House to do it. He was so elevated about it that he said it would be sacrilege to use that palette again, and he had the case made and put the palette inside with his own hands and then had the thing screwed up."

"They did take themselves seriously, didn't they?" said Susan, and Virgilia replied:

"A defect of their period; they mattered more than their art. I asked my father about this palette and he wandered on for quite a while. I understood him to say that he had some lines from the Tennyson 'Welcome to Alexandra' painted on the wall below the palette. They're not there now. My own belief is that Trimming had them painted over. Trimming was very jealous. Come and sit down, my dear. Mr. Raven, if you go into my so-called kitchen over there, you'll find a bottle of sherry and a corkscrew. I found the sherry in the old wine chest in the dining-room, and it's probably good sherry, though it may have deteriorated through age. Will you bring some glasses in and let us sample it?"

"That'll be marvellous," said Peter, and Virgilia added:

"Of course I asked the policemen if I might have it, and they were very courteous about it. Oh, dear, how ridiculous it all is!"

2

"My dear child, I'm so exasperated over the whole thing I feel I should like to go and smash all the windows at the police station, like the suffragettes when I was young," declared Virgilia.

"I'm so glad you feel like that, Miss Delafield," said Peter Raven. "It shows it's not getting you down. If you decide to smash the windows, do let me come and help. I should love to."

"Very civil of you," said Virgilia. "What does get me down is realising how much intelligence is being wasted by our police force. The Scotland Yard man is a very intelligent fellow, and a very pleasant one. There are plenty of real problems on which the police could well exercise their talents, and here they are, concentrating on poor crazy Trimming tripping over a stair rod with the supper tray. And why? All because that wretched plasterer can't be found. If they'd only seen the man—old, decrepit, bow-legged, mumbling. Roy's quite right when he says Trimming could have thrown him out of a window with one hand tied behind her."

She spoke quickly, incisively, with a vigour that was remarkable from one of her old-fashioned academic aspect. Peter Raven was enjoying her, and he hoped she would go on talking.

"It must be very irritating for you to have your work interrupted," he put in diplomatically.

"It's maddening," she said. "I can't even concentrate on proof-reading, because every time I get started I expect another policeman to come and inquire into my life story. And what my life story has to do with Trimming falling downstairs I cannot fathom.

Ah, here is Roy. Roy, come and try the sherry. It's very good, a really dry Amontillado; much better than I should have expected father to buy. I gather he liked sweet sherry—a drink I dislike quite excessively."

"Hallo. How nice of you to come," said Roy, with a smile for Susan and a nod towards Peter, who responded in kind. "Fancy the Ancient having some decent sherry... Yes, please, from me... Do you think there's likely to be any more in the wine cellar? He did have a wine cellar, didn't he?"

"All gentlemen's houses of that period had wine cellars," replied Virgilia. "Though I doubt very much if there'll be anything left in it. Father liked wine, but you can't indulge such a taste on a housekeeping allowance of five pounds a week."

"If there's any left, let's drink it before the landlord distrains," said Roy. He turned to Susan. "When the C.I.D. chap told me about the Ancient having won thousands in a lottery, I had an upsurge of optimism. It'd be marvellous to find there were a few thousand hidden away because the old boy had forgotten all about them. After all, he was practically gaga when Trimming hauled him home from the beaches, and it's quite conceivable he never remembered quite what he had got."

"Really, Roy, I think it's time you gave up harping on that topic," said Virgilia tartly. "I don't mean any disrespect to your uncle, my dear," she added to Susan; "but I think he must be mistaken on that point. It seems to me quite wildly improbable. Roy's mother saw my father not very long after 1926, and she would certainly have heard about the lottery had he won it. People would have talked—they always do."

"I don't know," said Roy. "Perhaps he managed to keep quiet about it, so that people shouldn't pester him for money. He was hideously mean. I'm prepared to believe Mr. Truby's right in what he says. After all, he's a very accurate person, isn't he?" he added to Susan.

"Yes. He is; and he has a very good memory. I'm sure he's right in what he says," replied Susan.

"But if he had a large inflow of capital, wouldn't his bank still have the records of it?" inquired Peter Raven.

"The great idea is that he kept two quite separate banking accounts, one in England, one in France," said Roy. "And it's quite possible he had more than one account in France. Anyway, if there's anything in it, the C.I.D. will rout it out. That's the one advantage of the whole mess-up. The C.I.D. will do all the work over making the French banks cough up information, and it'd have been a labour of Hercules for any ordinary person to get anything out of a French bank. So perhaps it'll run to a nice marble angel for Trimming's grave—in gratitude, and all that. Because if she hadn't come a cropper on the stairs the matter would never have come to the notice of the C.I.D."

"Would she have liked an angel?" asked Susan.

"She'd have preferred a devil with pincers, dealing faithfully with the non-saved," said Roy; "but I don't expect the cemetery authorities would have cared for that one. So it'd better be Angels Unawares."

"Then you don't think there's anything in the theory that Trimming looted whatever it was?" asked Peter.

Miss Virgilia turned on him at once. "Let me make this quite clear," she said. "I described Trimming as mad. To my mind, the description was justified, because she was a religious maniac. With the best intentions in the world she would have terrorised over a very old man with her lurid visions of hell. But I never suggested, even when I was most exasperated with her, that she was other than devoted to my father. Trimming would never have stolen from him—never. I am so sure of that that any theory which impugns her honesty is rubbish so far as I am concerned."

"Hats off to Trimming, or giving the devil his due," said Roy. "I agree with Auntie V. over this. But I wish we could find that blighted plasterer. It's Wally who's gone with the wind."

"It does seem queer that he has disappeared," said Susan, and Virgilia replied:

"Queer? My dear, it's maddening! And I feel I ought to be able to remember something about him. You see, my father spoke of him as though he were somebody he knew—had known for a long time."

"When Mr. Delafield told Trimming to get Walter to come, how would Trimming have got in touch with Walter?" asked Peter.

Roy looked at Peter suspiciously and said: "How do you know about Walter, anyway?"

Susan said hastily: "Because we've all been talking about it—Jocelyn and myself, and Peter because he came here that day. I'm terribly sorry if you think it's awful of us, but we can't help being interested."

"My dear, of course you're interested," said Virgilia. "Don't imagine I mind you talking about it, and nobody could have been kinder than your uncle has been. He has already made inquiries with the Portington estate about this lease, and all the worries I foresee in connection with it." She turned to Peter. "I think your question a very cogent one; I had considered the matter myself. As you know, there is no telephone here, and as far as I know—and the tradespeople can tell me—Trimming never used a telephone. I imagine she would have got my father to write a postcard—not a letter, that would have been wasting a halfpenny. Although his sight was very poor, he could still write fairly clearly, as his cheques testify, and he certainly addressed the envelopes for his cheques to be posted in. The rates and taxes and the larger outgoings were paid by cheque. As for Walter's address—of which the police can find no trace—Trimming would have known it. She had the sort of memory which retained addresses indefinitely."

"How tiresome of her," said Peter unreasonably, but Miss Delafield agreed with him at once.

"That's just it. She *was* tiresome. I feel she might well be laughing at us, because she has made things so difficult. She was, as Roy has said, a secret sort of person. It gave her a feeling of power to be the sole repository of information. She must have destroyed all my father's old papers and letters, and even books. That's why it's so difficult for the police to find out all the details they feel they ought to know."

"So far as the books are concerned, I bet she burnt them in the boiler," said Roy. "She thought all books pertained to the devil—save the One and Only. Trimming was a real fundamentalist. In addition to which, her craze for economy would have delighted in saving a penn'orth of coal by burning all the combustible matter she could lay hands on."

"Gosh! Do you think she would have burnt the securities or scrip or whatever you call it?" put in Susan. "If she'd a craze for burning things and was bats anyway, she might have gone through Mr. Delafield's desk and just burnt anything without telling him."

Roy gave a howl of woe. "Hell and Hades! Don't be so harsh. I can't bear to think of it. But there's bound to be records. I simply cling to the thought of records, like Trimming to the 'Rock of Ages.' You see, the C.I.D.'ll rout things out. If there's anything in the lottery racket, they'll get on the trail. I'm pinning my hopes to the C.I.D."

3

"It does seem mean that poor Miss Virgilia's being so worried," said Susan.

They had gone out into the garden and were sitting on the parapet of the non-existent well. "This place could be heaven for her if only the police would clear out. She could get rid of all the pictures and we'd paint the studio for her—all chaste and white with a green ceiling—and she could write great works in peace. She could let the house furnished and tell the landlords to go and boil their heads when the lease peters out. I'm sure it'd be all right. Ground landlords aren't all that powerful in these days of the welfare state." She looked round the overgrown garden and turned to Peter. "Didn't you say you learned to scythe when you went harvesting in Derbyshire that time, because a scythe's what's needed here."

"Here, dash it all, I could wield a scythe," said Roy. "I've never suggested it, because of Trimming. She used to bury her cats here and she didn't want them disturbed."

"I wonder if she buried anything else," suggested Peter, but Susan put in:

"We've counted that out. Miss Virgilia swears Trimming was honest, and when a woman hates another one as much as Miss Virgilia hated Trimming, you can be sure she's right about the hated one being honest."

"It's a wonderful sentence; I wondered how you were going to get it finished," said Peter.

"Look here. About Wally the plasterer," said Susan. "Couldn't we do anything to find out about him? I'm awfully good at asking people questions; it's all a matter of being polite. People will tell you anything if you only ask them nicely."

"It's no go, Sue," said Peter. "The police are asking the questions. It's an awful mistake to imagine the police are incompetent, because they're not."

"I never said they were," she retorted; "but there's competence and competence. I believe the coalman and the milkman and the fishmonger would tell me all sorts of things they'd never tell the police. And I could go into the local draper where Trimming bought her darning wool and have a heart to heart with the girl behind the counter in a way no policeman could. And once you get talking over the haberdashery in a small draper's shop, there's no end to what's told you. I know. You don't."

Roy began to laugh, but Peter Raven scowled. His long lean face, pale under the dark hair which tended to get untidy when the wind ruffled it, could be a charming gentle face, especially when he looked at Susan, but it altered surprisingly when he got irritable.

"Snap out of it, Sue. It's a rotten idea. You can't go round asking haberdashers questions. This is a criminal case."

"Who says so?" she flashed back. "You might as well say you're a criminal when the police stop you for speeding in a built-up area. They're doing their job as police; and that's what they're doing here. And it's not your business to tell me what I can do and what I can't do."

"Hear, hear," said Roy. "Feminine emancipation; I'm all in favour of it. I only wish I could have heard Auntie V. telling the Chief Inspector where he got off when he suggested she couldn't recognise her own father. But if you do go and talk to the female who sells darning wool and stockings and what have you, what'd you ask her?"

"Oh, I should just lead her on," replied Susan. "After all, Trimming had to buy stockings somewhere—they're things you simply must buy—and whoever sold them to her was bound to be intrigued, because she must have looked wonderful. What sort of stockings did she wear?"

"Black ones," said Roy promptly. "I should like to say black woollen ones, but I never got near enough to see."

"Black—she may have dyed them," murmured Susan; "but I could find out. Stockings are a good topic to start on, anyway. And then with the fishmonger I could talk about cats. If Trimming was fond of her cat she'd have got cod's head or other horrors for it, and if she was so jolly economical she'd have cadged odd bits and pieces after she'd bought Dover sole for the master. Black stockings and cods' heads are both nice confidence-making topics, and no detective would ever use them as stepping-off places."

"I think you'd be jolly good at it," said Roy; "but will it get you any nearer to Wally?"

"It might. If *you* went and talked to them, they'd know you were an interested party and they'd be cagey accordingly, and if the police did they'd watch their step in case they're run in for making false statements. Everybody's careful what they say to policemen; weren't you?"

"Well, I started off by meaning to be careful, but Rivers, the C.I.D. bloke, was so much like a human being that I forgot as I went along and just talked," replied Roy.

Peter was sitting silent, staring across the garden, and Susan suddenly felt contrite because she'd snapped at him. After all, he'd driven her here, and he'd been very nice to Miss Virgilia.

"Well, leaving my ideas out of it, how would you start if you were looking for a lost plasterer?" she inquired. "Let's pool ideas. Peter, you've always got ideas."

His dark head came round, as it nearly always did when Susan tried, but he still sounded irritable.

"I'm not likely to have any ideas the C.I.D. won't have thought about first," he said. "This sort of thing is their job, they know the technique. I expect they started with the fact that the bloke pushed a barrow or trolley; he didn't come in a van. And he was an old chap, so he couldn't have been expected to come very far. I'd put three miles as the outside limit."

"I don't know," said Roy. "The chaps from Covent Garden and the ordinary barrow boys shove their outfits a heck of a way. But if you only take a radius of three miles from here, you get a surprisingly big area to search. Think it out. Three miles would get you down to Westminster in the south and towards Hampstead in the north—right out to Golders Green and Highgate Archway, wouldn't it; and westwards? Lord, it'd take you nearly to Wormwood Scrubs and certainly to Hammersmith, and east as far as St. Paul's, with all the Holborn area and Covent Garden and Long Acre and Soho…"

"All right," said Peter. "I expect three miles is too large a radius. Call it two."

"Well, you still leave plenty of scope for fun and games with a two-mile radius," said Roy. "That'd include the working-class area of Paddington and Notting Hill and Harrow Road and Bayswater. There must be thousands of old codgers with barrows in those areas alone. It'll take the police about six months of Sundays to comb all that for antique plasterers, and Wally may fall down dead before they get to him."

Susan laughed, and the sound of her laughter did nothing to cheer up Peter.

"Perhaps my way might be best after all," she said. "I always distrust people who start with given radii. I was never any good at geometry. Hallo… Who's this?"

The drawing-room window was pushed open and a tall man stepped on to the terrace.

"It's Rivers," said Roy. "The Scotland Yard bloke. Is he going to get fresh because we've come into the garden?"

4

Far from being difficult, Rivers was his most urbane. Roy introduced him and he bowed to Susan with a smile which wasn't any different from the smiles she generally succeeded in evoking.

"I do hope it's all right about us coming out here, Chief Inspector," she said. "It's so lovely, even though the garden is all wild."

"It's perfectly all right so far as my department is concerned," he replied, "and I agree that it's lovely—including the wildness. The sight of you all looking so happy and carefree made me take a sudden dislike to the dusty job which duty thrust upon me in there."

"But we are being very serious," said Susan, with an impish impulse to take the bull by the horns. "We were discussing radii. Would you like to give us your professional opinion on the probable distance an aged plasterer would manhandle a barrow to oblige an old customer?"

Rivers laughed. "I'm not really an expert on this, Miss Truby. Some of the point-duty men and traffic police would make a much more authoritative estimate. Also, I'm not really a pedestrian. My private opinion is a mile to a mile and a half—and even that is quite a haystack in terms of London."

"This chap suggested three miles," grinned Roy, indicating Peter, but Rivers replied:

"It's not impossible, you know. It's like wheeling a pram. I know several energetic matrons who say they can walk miles with a pram; it gives them something to lean on, whereas they weary in half a mile if they've got nothing to push."

Peter suddenly grinned. "I like that," he said. "But the size of the job, even cutting the radius down to a mile and a half, simply appals me. Do you round up all the barrows, trolleys and whatnots in a given area?"

"No. It's not quite like that," said Rivers. "You'd be surprised how much the point-duty men know about the working inhabitants of their areas."

"Now say if you find an aged plasterer who seems to coincide with the not-very-precise description given," said Roy, "and assume that he says, 'Not me, mister. Never heard of the qualified house.' And further assume that when you show him to us we exclaim with one voice, '*That* is the man; *that* is our Walter.' Whom do you believe?"

"None of you," retorted Rivers.

"We have our methods, Watson," retorted the irrepressible Roy. "I expect the poor old codger left his fingerprints all over the drawing-room."

"That may be very useful to sort him out when they've found him, but I don't suppose it really gets them anywhere while they're still looking for him, does it?" Susan demanded of Rivers.

"No. Not unless the fingerprints have previously been recorded by the police," said Rivers, "and not always then."

"Oh, dear. It does sound chancey," she said. "*Do* find him. It's so miserable for poor Miss Virgilia, and if you only got it all tidied up, we've got lovely plans for moving the pictures out and leaving her in peace to write her books in a reconstituted studio."

"We're doing our best," said Rivers, and he spoke soberly.

"Would you like us to lend a hand in looking for the plasterer?" asked Peter.

Rivers turned and looked at him. "Where do you come in?" he asked. It was Susan who answered:

"We're just friends of the family. You've met my Uncle Jocelyn, haven't you? You see, we all want to help."

Rivers turned from Peter Raven and studied Susan instead. "That's a very friendly neighbourly thing to say," he replied; "but I should leave it alone if I were you. You may get in somebody's way."

"Your way?"

"Not of necessity. Though if you do, you won't get any preferential treatment from me—any of you. I'm afraid it's our job, and we've got to go through with it."

"But I should love to beat you to it," smiled Susan.

XI

I

"The fact is, folks hexaggerate. Give 'em a good story and they make it better," said Mr. Jenks. "'Uman nature's like that," he observed.

Mr. Jenks, if not the oldest inhabitant in the neighbourhood of the Delafields' house, could boast eighty-odd years, and he had once worked in the garden of Firenze. A constable of D Division had produced Mr. Jenks for Rivers's consideration, and Rivers had called to see him in his small house near the old cemetery. Jenks was able to give a more reasonable account of Trimming than anybody else had achieved to date.

"From the horphanage she came, sir. Salem, they called it, and it was a big house which was pulled down when them flats was put up by Lords. Very 'arsh they was to horphans in those days. They wore long black capes and bonnets, pore young things, and when they walked out, two by two, they had to fold their hands in front under their cloaks and keep their eyes on the ground. Miss Maria Bull, she run the place, and paid for it, too, being wealthy. Religious, she was. Took the horphans to a chapel nearby—great ugly place, it was, built o' yellow brick. Salem's Tabernacle, they called it, and them horphans went to service three times a day on Sunday and the sermons was hours long, I'm told. It shut down years ago, there being not enough folks to keep it up. 'Salem's 'Osts,' they called themselves. Sort of 'ot Gospellers, very strong on the devil. 'Twas said they chased the devil round and round that chapel."

Mr. Jenks paused after his fine descriptive effort and then added: "But Miss Bull, she made good maidservants o' them female horphans. Never had no trouble over placing them in good service."

Mr. Jenks looked at Rivers with eyes which were still shrewd. "If a youngster's brought up in a horphanage like that one was, never knowing no kith nor kin and talked to about devils with 'orns and tails—well, it's not to be wondered at if she goes queer. And Miss Trimming was queer; I'll say that. But not so queer as folks made out."

"Do you remember Mr. Adrian Delafield?" asked Rivers.

"Bless you, yes. I often had a word with him in the old days; very 'andsome gentleman, 'e was—but close. Argue over an 'alfpenny change, 'e would—and Miss Trimming, too."

"Were you in the district when Mr. Delafield and Trimming came back to Firenze in 1940?" asked Rivers.

"Yes, I was. Never budged, not right through the blitz. And I went to the 'ouse, too, and lent an 'and getting things straight, the drains and gutters being in a bad way, and doors and windows stuck, though the 'ouse was never damaged."

"Did Mr. Delafield send for you?" asked Rivers.

"Not 'im. Very poorly, 'e was. Miss Trimming she came knockin' on my door one day and said, 'Jenks, we need some work done,' and knowing 'ow difficult it was to get an 'and's turn from anyone them days, I went along to oblige. I saw the old gent, too. In bed 'e was, and I 'ad to get the chimney cleared in 'is room so's they could light a fire. And see 'ere, sir: Miss Trimming, she worked like an 'ero getting that 'ouse shipshape, and no mistake about it. Queer she might've been, and I'm not denying it, but she was a proper worker."

Rivers then asked Mr. Jenks if he could remember anything about the so-called "minister of religion" who came to wrestle for Mr. Delafield's soul after the return from France. Rivers had been nursing a theory that the "minister" might turn out to be identical with the plasterer. But this notion was speedily put paid to by Mr. Jenks.

"Minister? Chap in shabby black and a shovel 'at? Now I know 'im, funnily enough; or I should say knew. Proper nuisance' e was. You see, I caught sight of 'im when I was there clearing them drains in the area. A leftover, 'e was; one o' the chaps used to go to Salem's Tabernacle as a boy. He got in the way of preachin', and I've seen 'im on a tub at Marble Arch. 'Armless, but barmy. Kept hisself by addressing envelopes for one of them dotty societies what sent out stuff about the pyramids—prophecies and lost tribes and that. Very poor, 'e was. I reckon Miss Trimming gave him a decent meal when he came to do 'is stuff. 'E lived in Watson's Rents, off Lisson Grove, and 'e was run over by a lorry last month. Died in Paddington 'Orspital. I 'eard of it at the pub; 'Ell Fire 'Enery, they called 'im."

Mr. Jenks gave a deep chuckle. "Never understood religion meself; never taken that way; but I can see why Trimming got 'Enery along to the old gentleman. She was simple that way, and so was 'Enery—well meaning, I dessay, but simple. And if you'd been brought up in a horphanage like Miss Trimming was, and taken to 'ear Salem's 'Osts on Sundays, maybe it'd've done something to you like it did to her."

Rivers was interested in the old man's trend. He said: "You really liked Miss Trimming, didn't you?"

"I wouldn't say liked, sir. She wasn't a person you liked. But I saw her workin' and lookin' after the old gent single-'anded. And I respected 'er for it. She was a good worker an' a first-rate cook, an' she could 'ave made good money, with a comfortable room and wireless an' all the hanky-panky the cooks expect these days.

And she stayed there, workin' for the old gent till she died. And there's not many like 'er these days, as you'll agree. Do as little as you can for as much money as you can get—that's to-day's motto."

On the subject of the plasterer Mr. Jenks was unable to give any information at all, though he hazarded the suggestion (already put forward by Miss Virgilia) that "Walter" had worked for the firm which had built the covered way.

"A firm of builders in Pimlico, it was," said Jenks; "but they went out o' business years ago. Special stuff, they did, hartistic and that; them mosaics and ornamental brickwork and tiling. Went out o' fashion—or people couldn't afford fancy stuff any longer. But I'll say this, sir. Miss Trimming, she was hold-fashioned; liked chaps such as me who treated 'er proper and didn't get arguing they knew best. If so be she wanted a plasterer, she'd've got someone she knew."

Rivers finally elicited the fact that the last time Mr. Jenks had been at Firenze was in 1946, when he cut back some shrubs. In 1947 he had broken his thigh bone, and though it mended, his active days were over.

Dowding had produced the list of tradespeople where Trimming did her shopping. These were all small shops owned by the shopkeepers themselves. The grocer, an intelligent man of sixty, had given an account of Trimming as he knew her. She came to the shop early, generally on Monday morning, carrying two large baskets; she knew exactly what she wanted though she never had a list. She ordered from memory and knew exactly what things cost. She paid cash, and always asked for a receipted bill. When asked if Trimming had been able to read the bill, the grocer admitted he had often wondered.

"She knew her numbers," he said. "She could read prices and she could tot up; added on her fingers, she did, and never made a mistake. But the last year or so she got more and more short-sighted. I doubt if she could see the labels on the tins across the counter, but she could see things close to, all right. She'd stick her face near to mine, and I once said: 'You could do with some spectacles ma'am,' and I've always remembered her answer: 'I don't hold with such vanities.' I often wonder she didn't get run over, because she couldn't see a thing more than a yard away. I reckon she was too close to pay for specs, even the quid or so they charge you on National Health."

"Was she insured?" asked Dowding.

"Not she. Over sixty, so she could choose for herself, and she'd never have wasted money on the stamps."

2

Rivers and Lancing met in Firenze the same evening that Susan and Peter and Roy had been in the garden. Lancing said, "What cheer?" and Rivers replied:

"None whatever, so far as the case is concerned. It all seems cut and dried. Trimming is given the best of characters by everybody, apart from her tendency to enlarge on hell fire. She was so short-sighted she was liable to trip over anything, and it seems highly questionable if she could read or write at all. If that's true, she couldn't have done any funny stuff with documents or other securities, and it explains why she hadn't any papers of her own. And there's not even a *Mrs. Beeton* in the kitchen; no cookery book of any kind."

"And no sign of Wally, the plasterer?"

"None; but since I've seen old Jenks, I'm wondering if that's as significant as it seemed at first. If Trimming got hold of some very old codger to do the job, it's just possible that he may not read the papers and therefore knows nothing about the shemozzle here; and it's also possible she paid him in cash by the day. It's the sort of thing she liked doing. Anyway, since nothing appears to be missing from the house, there's no case the D.P.P. would consider a case—unless Henry Fearon digs something up in France. He flew over yesterday, and he's got the Sureté behind him to ensure that the banks will give him facilities." Rivers looked around the gloomy dining-room, where they sat. "Bradey and I have been all over the house; it's a blameless house. Everything is here that ought to be here, including the few papers that Delafield kept in his own desk. It's true that there's a marked lack of reading matter, but as his eyes were too weak for him to read, there's nothing surprising in that."

"Both of them as blind as bats," murmured Lancing. "Anything in that? With the rotten light on the stairs, anybody could have hidden by that turn and given Trimming an almighty shove with a broom or something, to cause what Dowding called 'additional velocity.'"

"Of course they could," agreed Rivers. "I agree that this could have been the simplest sort of murder, but it's no use postulating that somebody murdered the woman unless you can provide a motive to support the theory. And so far we haven't got any support from any motive. Now tell me about your private researches."

"Mr. Truby and friends," said Lancing. "I thought it was worth spending some time on Truby because he's one of the few people who seemed to link up. He knew Delafield in the past, and he'd been here to see him." He stopped for a moment, considering, and then went on: "It's worth remembering that if Mr. Truby is not as truthful as he appears to be, it would have been possible for him to have paid what visits he liked to this house, unknown to anybody but Trimming. He could have come to the front door and nobody would have noticed him."

"Yes. I grant you that," said Rivers; "but it's hypothetical, and on the face of it improbable. If he'd been exploring avenues here, for the purpose of getting away with the loot, whatever the loot was, I don't think he'd have told us about Delafield winning a lottery. That implied that there might be a source of valuables, and if Truby was cashing in on the possibility, would he have told us about it?"

"I'm not so sure," said Lancing slowly. "Truby's been taking an interest; and he got himself asked to the house. He may have argued, quite intelligently, that the lottery money would come to light somehow, and he'd be in a better position if he'd drawn attention to it and progged us into thinking that the plasterer had got away with it, via Trimming."

Rivers began to laugh. "You'll be suggesting that Truby was the plasterer next."

"I'd suggest anything rather than accept stalemate," said Lancing. "The only objection to that theory is that the plasterer was working here when Truby came to tea."

"Although nobody saw him on that occasion because he was in the kitchen having a cuppa with Trimming, and Trimming's dead," said Rivers. "But a much more insuperable difficulty is that Miss Virgilia saw the plasterer and said he looked like a moron. I've already asked Miss Virgilia if she was satisfied that her father *was* her father; if I ask her if the plasterer could have been Truby, she'll complain to the Home Secretary, the Commissioner and the P.M."

"That was Truby's idea—about Delafield not being Delafield," said Lancing, and Rivers nodded.

"An extremely ingenious idea, too. He challenged me to prove—or disprove—his idea. Well, happily the proof exists. Have you thought that one out?"

Lancing nodded. "Yes. Are you leaving it in situ?"

"I am, for the moment. If anybody obliges by tampering with evidence we shall begin to get a move on. At the moment everybody is behaving perfectly. Now, don't tell me you haven't got anything but suspicions of Jocelyn Truby to show for your day's work. I could have boiled that up without moving a finger."

"Oh, I've been getting round, developing a background to Truby, plus his young friends. There's this chap named Raven who seems to be taking an interest," said Lancing.

"Yes. He was here this afternoon, in the garden," replied Rivers, "taking an interest, as you say, but I thought it was in Truby's niece."

"So I'm told. All in the family, as one might say. What interests me is that he's been seen waffling around in this neighbourhood, even around these walls—and I should like to know why. He lives in Chelsea, and this is right off his beat. Also he was in the army with Roy Delafield—Field Security, both of them."

"Waffling around," said Rivers. "You're waffling yourself. Who saw him and where?"

"Dowding saw Raven's car parked in the studio cul-de-sac a week before Trimming was killed. The car was empty. He was seen in a pub—the Blenheim—four nights later; that's only ten minutes away from here, and in the same pub the night after Trimming was killed. He's an extravagant bloke, and I'm told he's in debt all round. Query, did Truby get chatting one day and give Raven the impression that this house was worth looting?"

Rivers sat and pondered. "I don't want to turn down a suggestion because it's improbable," he said slowly. "We've met some improbabilities in our time, and they have seemed quite crazy until a single factor emerged which made them seem obvious—and then everything clicked. I'm prepared to admit that there have been occasions when a young man like Raven, or an old one like Truby, have taken a chance when they saw what they thought was easy money, and have become murderers in the process. But in considering them, you've got to take all factors into consideration. Now say if you repeat everything that you regard as essential in this case."

"First, that the murderer must have been in the house," said Lancing. "If Trimming was murdered, it must have been by the simple expedient of giving her an almighty shove from behind; a booby-trap like a trip cord would have brought her down, but not of necessity killed her. A real shove, with weight behind it, would have crashed her clear down, and the floor in the hall is tiled. Her own weight broke her neck, because she fell on her head, but her skull was fractured, too. I think it could be reckoned a cert if she was shoved hard enough, because that flight of stairs is a long one because the rooms are so tall."

"Yes. I agree with you there," said Rivers. "And then—?"

"Then the murderer took whatever it was—presumably from Trimming's room. I think it would have been in Trimming's room, because that's the one room no one would ever go into. Miss Delafield sometimes looked into the other rooms, but not into Trimming's—doctrine of non-interference again."

"Yes. All right. We won't argue over that—though I should like to know how the murderer knew the doings were there. I agree with Roy Braithwaite's idea that Trimming wasn't likely to have confided her secrets to anybody. And then? How did the murderer get out?"

"Well, I postulated that he could have stayed in the house and got out when Longaby and Miss Delafield went upstairs; but that wouldn't have worked for Truby or Raven. They couldn't have risked being out of evidence half the morning—and Raven was at his job before ten, anyway."

"Yes. Still a question mark," said Rivers, "and the only questionable character we've got is the plasterer, inasmuch as he's one large question mark. I still think he's the crux. You can say he supplied the explanation as well as the question mark."

Lancing nodded. "The explanation being that the crash of the plaster falling gave Trimming such a shock she fell downstairs. And if that wasn't enough to satisfy us, the non-existent plasterer could take the blame."

"That's about it," said Rivers. "That's why I'm convinced there's something phony here. We're being offered an either/or. Now let's concentrate on the plasterer again. I should be quite willing to believe the plasterer had been murdered, too. But we nearly always get a report if somebody disappears; even an old man living alone is missed. The neighbours or the landlady or the milkman notice he hasn't shown up."

Again Lancing nodded. There had been no report of a traffic accident or a hospital case; no body found by the river police, no unidentified corpse found anywhere in the country; no "missing man" reported to any station.

"It brings us back to the most obvious answer," said Lancing slowly. "Have we tried to be too smart? We asked ourselves, 'What had Trimming got in the way of valuables?' and tried to connect it up with lottery winnings and loot on a large scale. Perhaps the answer is intended theft on a small scale. The plasterer meant to pinch the silver spoons and somehow he got caught at it by Trimming and shoved her downstairs."

"Only we know that won't wash," said Rivers disgustedly. "As Miss Delafield observed quite cogently, a burglar had only got to wait until Trimming was in bed and asleep to pinch the spoons with impunity. And the spoons were downstairs anyway, while Trimming was shoved from upstairs. There's another point which I don't swallow, in addition. The thing was timed for us."

"The clock in the drawing-room?" asked Lancing.

"Yes. Why was the clock in the drawing-room at all? The ceiling had been finished—and it's worth while noting that a plasterer *had* been at work, and done his job with reasonable competence, even though the ceiling fell later. The room had been cleaned—all the paintwork had been washed and the windows cleaned by Trimming. There's enough of her fingerprints to show she did the job. But would she have put the clock back on the shelf before she'd got the pictures up and the other junk back? I don't think she would. I think the clock was put there as a demonstration that the plaster fell at the same time that Trimming did. And that leads me to my last point. I believe the plaster fell because the chap who did it intended it to fall. He organised it so that a bang on the floor above or a prod between the boards upstairs would bring it down."

"Well, that simply means the plasterer did the whole show."

"Not of necessity. The plasterer may have worked in collaboration with someone else—two of them at it. And that leads to the idea that the plasterer himself was phony."

Lancing pondered and then—always ready with a guess to fit the problem—suggested: "Understudy for Walter? Another chap coming along with apologies for Walter, the latter being ill... But it's damned complicated to see how it was worked."

"I'm beginning to believe it *was* worked," said Rivers. "But who in this set-out was the plasterer beats me; we haven't anybody for the part. And there are two questions which still go milling round and round. Why kill Trimming and leave old Delafield alive? And how the hell did the murderer get out of the house? I don't think we've got the answer to either of those yet."

"My bet is that old Delafield was left alive because he could have given evidence that Trimming fell downstairs. He didn't see it happen, but he'd have heard it and it must have sounded pretty convincing," said Lancing, "and following your theory that the plaster was left ready to fall at a touch, wouldn't the crash and shake-up made by Trimming's fall be enough to bring it down if it was very unstable?"

"Quite likely," said Rivers; "but you still haven't answered the second question. The only window Dowding found open was the bedroom window, and Longaby said that was latched and secure when he pulled the curtains back. Everything else was latched, bolted or chained. What have we missed?"

Lancing looked round the dreary room. Twilight was falling, but there was no mantle on the incandescent gas fitment.

"Let's go round the whole place again to-morrow," he said. "It's no go to-night; we can't see a thing in this blighted house. Let's give it best for to-night—and concentrate on possible collaborators to-morrow."

XII

I

IT WAS ACTUALLY WHILE RIVERS AND LANCING WERE DEBATING their problems in the depressing and deepening gloom of the dining-room at Firenze, that a big car bucketed down Praed Street towards Paddington Station at a speed which was certainly over that permitted by the law in a built-up area.

At this time in the evening, between seven and eight o'clock, all traffic was able to move faster than at any time in the day since the early morning. The rush hour was over; tradesmen's vans and the majority of lorries were no longer on the road, and private cars were at a minimum, for their owners were eating dinner—or supper—according to their habits. The shops had closed and even the vendors of evening papers were having an easy. Constable Brown saw the car pass him; it was a big grey car with nobody but the driver in it, and Brown noticed automatically that it was speeding a bit, but the road was clear and Brown was accustomed to drivers who made up for lost time once they had passed the traffic lights at the Edgware Road crossing. He got a vague impression of the registration number, but not of the make of the car, and his attention was distracted by a stray dog which looked as though it ought to be taken in charge, for it had no collar and was in wretched condition. Brown was deciding what to do about the dog when he heard a scream some distance in front of him; it was a loud frightened scream, and Brown left the dog and hurried off to investigate the scream.

At the corner of London Street a group of people had materialised in the uncanny way that people always collect in London streets when something out of the way happens. Brown expected to find a brawl (it was a district where fights were not uncommon in the evenings), but he realised what had happened before he reached the corner. A crumpled body lay in the gutter and the woman who had screamed was holding forth at the top of her voice.

"It's plain murder; 'e must 'ave seen 'im. 'E came round the corner on the pavement as fast as an express train and 'e'd have got me, too, if I 'adn't jumped to it."

It was a sadly familiar story, and Brown was busy for the next few minutes doing the routine jobs of the occasion. With the help of an off-duty porter from Paddington Station he lifted the body on to the pavement; it was that of an old man, clad in the dreary shoddy garments of the poor. The porter (a responsible sort of chap) went to telephone the police, and Brown produced his notebook to enter the names of witnesses. At the sight of the notebook the majority of them decided they'd seen nothing and had urgent business elsewhere. The woman who had screamed stood her ground and became voluble over what she had witnessed. She gave her name and address as Mrs. Murphy of Spring Street; her story (shorn of its redundancies) was that she had seen the old man standing on the pavement close by the gutter, as though he were nervous of crossing the road, and a big blue car had come down Praed Street, turned left at London Street, cutting the corner so that its wheels mounted the pavement, and it had run down the old man and crashed him to the ground. "And never stopped," declared Mrs. Murphy; "just roared off faster than ever, leaving me leaning by the wall. Fair sick it turned me."

"A blue car?" asked the policeman. "Are you sure it wasn't grey?"

"Blue," she reiterated. "I saw it, didn't I? Near as not killed me, too."

"I reckon it was green," said another onlooker; "dark green, and it was a big car, one o' them American makes, I reckon. Want the whole road to themselves."

Brown was accustomed to differences of opinion among witnesses. As a matter of form, he asked if anybody had seen the registration number, though he knew from experience that when witnessses had been frightened by the sight of a horrifying accident, they very seldom noticed car numbers—it was all over too quickly. His experience proved right—the testimony about the car registration was as variable as that about its colour. In any case, as somebody pointed out, the light was awkward—it was neither light nor dark.

It was just as the ambulance came up that a newspaper vendor volunteered a statement after looking at the pallid old face of the victim.

"That's old Potts," he said. "Lives in a shack back o' Lisson Grove, behind that old furniture shop—second-hand stuff. You'll find that's 'oo 'e is. Poor ole Potts. Told me 'e'd backed a winner or some such. 'A bit o' fat,' he said. Maybe 'e put down one too many on 'is winnings and didn't think to get out o' the way."

2

Poor old Potts wasn't dead, but the doctor in the "casualty" at the nearby hospital gave scant hope of his survival. "He may live the night," he said, "and it's barely possible he'll have a moment or two of consciousness before he goes—they do sometimes. If he's got a wife or anybody, send them along. They can stay with him—it won't be more than a few hours."

The Paddington Police notified the St. Marylebone Police (Lisson Grove was in the neighbouring borough to Paddington) and within an hour of the accident a constable of D Division was knocking at the side door of the second-hand furniture shop off Lisson Grove. The owner—name of Albert Edward Spragg—agreed that Potts lived on his premises.

"I let him have the room out at the back there," he said. "He only paid ten bob a week, but he was a useful old chap; sort of odd-job man, been in the building trade once, but he could turn his hand to anything. He'd often do repairs to stuff I bought cheap, and it suited us both."

It was the mention of "the building trade" which made the penny drop in the constable's mind. In common with all his mates, he had read the Yard "notices to all stations" inquiring about an old plasterer.

"In the building trade, eh? Had he got a barrow?"

"Not of his own. If he got an outside job he sometimes borrowed one of mine. I've got several in the yard—use 'em for moving small stuff. Potts'd do a bit of painting and papering sometimes. He'd got his pension, of course, but it's not much for a single chap to manage on."

"William Potts," echoed the constable. "Was he ever called Walter, or Wally?"

"Search me. We called him ole' Bill. And it's no manner of use your asking about his next of kin, because he hadn't any. Wife went in the blitz and his only son was drowned at Southend years ago."

"Was he out doing a job the last two weeks—Monday 29th to Tuesday 6th are the dates in question?"

"What are you getting at? Trying to make out Potts was a bad 'un—because I swear he wasn't."

"Don't you read the papers?"

"Only on Sundays, and not all that."

The constable did some heavy-handed explaining, and Albert Edward Spragg replied:

"Well, it's like this, mate. You're unlucky. I've been away, staying with my married daughter at St. Albans. There was two good sales there, in big old-fashioned houses, where you can pick job lots up cheap."

"But you didn't close the shop—I passed here and saw it open."

"Quite right. Ten to four. A neighbour obliged—Mrs. Wilton. But she wouldn't have taken any notice of Potts. Just stay behind the counter and answer inquiries till I come back, and sell anything that had its price marked."

After a few more inquiries the constable decided that this was a matter for higher authority. In the presence of Mr. Spragg, the arm of the law sealed old Potts's room and returned to make his report.

3

It was just half-past nine when D Division rang the Yard to report about old Potts. Rivers had gone home, but after some conversation D Division was given Rivers's private phone number, and there followed a careful verbal report about the accident in Praed Street, and about Potts's domicile and spare-time occupation. "We've got a man beside his bed, just in case," said D Division. "I don't know if you want to go along there, but the surgeon thinks the odds are against his recovering consciousness."

"O.K. Thanks a lot," said Rivers. "I'll get Lancing to go along and then I'll see how I get through with the chores."

Hanging up, Rivers sat and thought for the space of two minutes. The registration number of the car which knocked down Potts had had an M.E. or W.E. among its letters, according to Brown's recollection of it. Brown was certain that the car which did the damage must have been the one he saw in Praed Street. There had been no other big car which passed him in the time involved. Rivers went to his own lock-up, got his car out, and set out for Summer's Walk—the pleasantly named mews in Chelsea where Peter Raven lived. Peter's car had the registration letters XME, and it was an indeterminate grey-green in colour.

It had been eight o'clock when Potts was knocked down. It was a quarter past ten when Rivers arrived at Summer's Walk. The big car was parked neatly outside Peter Raven's window, close up against the wall. There was a light behind the curtained window and above the fanlight of the door, but Rivers did not ring the bell. He put his hand on the bonnet of the car to see if it was still warm. The bonnet was cold, but Rivers undid the catch, lifted the bonnet and put his hand on the radiator—it was warm, quite definitely warm.

It was at this juncture that Peter opened the door and demanded with some heat: "What the hell do you think you're doing?"

Rivers stood up, calmly let down the bonnet and replied: "I was seeing if the radiator was still warm. Can I come in?"

"If you want to. But why worry about my car?"

"The usual thing: report of a traffic accident and the suggestion that it was this car involved," said Rivers.

"I haven't had the car out all day," retorted Peter, but he held the door open for Rivers to walk through a tiny entrance lobby and on into the long, graceful, white room. The first thing he saw was Mr. Truby's comfortable figure, ensconced in Peter's most capacious chair. The old man was examining a small unframed canvas which he held balanced on his knees, and the expression of his chubby face as he looked up was frankly bewildered, whether by the picture or by the appearance of the Chief Inspector, it was impossible to say, but he soon recovered his usual urbanity.

"God bless my soul! This is an unexpected pleasure," said Jocelyn.

Peter Raven closed the door behind him and came forward into the room. "Perhaps it remains to be seen," he said. "It appears that the Chief Inspector has joined the traffic police; he seems to think I've been involved in a road accident."

Rivers said "Good evening" to Truby, and remained standing, since he hadn't been offered a chair. He turned to Peter, conscious of a slight sense of irritation that he had to look up at the young man's pale, slightly mocking face.

"You say that you haven't had the car out all day," he said, "but the radiator is still warm."

"Quite possibly. I ran the engine for some time when I came in, about six. The carburettor was misbehaving and the engine stalled when I pulled up. It's all right now."

"Then would you tell me what you have been doing during the course of the evening?"

"Not unless you give me good reason to do so. You say my car was involved in an accident. If so, where?"

"At the corner of Praed Street and London Street."

"Well, I wasn't there. I loathe Praed Street, anyway."

"And you're not prepared to say where you were?"

"Not unless you can tell me that my car was identified, without possibility of error, in the accident you're alluding to."

It was Mr. Truby who spoke next. "My dear boy, may I proffer a word of advice? An officer of the Chief Inspector's standing does not come and ask questions without very good grounds for doing so. After all, even though you were not driving the car, it's always possible that it might have been misappropriated. These things do happen."

"Let's alter the angle of the inquiry a little," said Rivers, and Truby said hastily:

"But sit down, Chief Inspector; sit down. After all, we're civilised beings—at least, I hope we are."

"I beg your pardon," said Peter stonily. "Please sit down."

Rivers said "Thanks," but remained standing, since Peter was doing so. "Do you habitually leave your car standing where it is now?" he asked.

"Yes. I do. It's a cul-de-sac, and nobody has ever raised any objections."

"I can assume you lock the car. Where do you keep the key?"

Peter produced the ignition key from his pocket.

"Have you got a spare one?"

"No."

"Have you ever had a spare one?"

There was a second's hesitation and then the young man said: "I had one, but it's got mislaid. I don't know exactly where it is now."

"Well, we're getting on," said Rivers. "I shall be able to bring a number of witnesses to have a look at the car, in order to identify it. An old man was knocked down, and he is now dying in hospital; a very serious charge will lie against the driver. Since you say you were not driving the car, I advise you strongly to make a statement as to your own whereabouts."

Jocelyn Truby intervened again here, in his reasonable, conciliatory way. "Surely it is being unwise, indeed obstructive, to refuse to give information to the police in such a case?"

Peter shrugged his shoulders and then replied: "All right. But I resent the easy assumption that my car, out of all the cars in London, caused this accident. If its number had been taken, the Chief Inspector would have said so at once. The number was obviously not taken; neither has he stated that the make of the car was recognised." With a rather shamefaced grin at Rivers, he added: "Shall we sit down? I don't want to obstruct the police, as Mr. Truby suggests; only to maintain the liberty of the subject."

"Having made your declaration of independence, say if you tell me what you were doing yourself this evening," said Rivers.

"I went out about a quarter to seven. I wanted to see the *Ulysses* film which is on at Marble Arch, so I went into the Cumberland for a sandwich and a drink, and then on to the cinema. I didn't like the film so I came out before it was half-through and got back here just after nine. The car was then in its usual place. Just as I got in, Mr. Truby rang me up; he wanted to look at that painting he's got there, and as he happened to be in the neighbourhood, he came in here shortly before you did."

"Thanks," said Rivers. "It seems a very innocent evening, and if somebody didn't notice you in the Cumberland I shall be surprised. You're definitely a few inches taller than the average."

After a moment's pause he went on: "It amounts to this: your car was standing out there for about two hours while you went to the cinema; plenty of time for it to have been driven to Praed Street and back several times over; and you say you 'mislaid' your second ignition key. Can't you be more specific over the key? Did it get lost in this flat, or did you drop it somewhere?"

"Neither. I gave it—or lent it—to a woman I know when we'd arranged to meet somewhere. I wasn't certain what time I could make it, and I said I'd park the car at the bottom of Waterloo Place and she could get in if she got there first. Actually, I got there first, and I forgot to ask her for the key back. When I did ask, she couldn't find it—and presumably she's still looking."

"And she probably dropped the key out of her bag or pocket while she was getting in or out of the car and it was picked up by somebody who recognised the car," suggested Jocelyn Truby. "Gross carelessness. It might have landed you in considerable trouble."

"'Might' is putting it mildly," said Peter Raven. "If nobody noticed me at the Cumberland and somebody swears they saw me driving the car, it looks like trouble all right—if your minions can swear to the car," he added to Rivers, and then continued with the faintly mocking expression so characteristic of him: "And since you came direct here like a homing pigeon, I take it you've got sworn evidence of some sort."

Rivers sat silent for a moment, looking at the oddly assorted pair in front of him—the tall, pale, dark young man and the plump, rubicund old one. Both very respectable and not undistinguished members of the professional classes—the classes least addicted to crime, and therefore the most difficult to bowl out, because it was so difficult to believe that crime was their line. As usual, he made his decision quickly, and said: "I'm quite prepared to tell you the facts of the case, and I shall be interested to have your comments—if you care to make any."

4

Deliberately pushing his chair back so that he faced both men squarely—the old man relaxed, almost benevolent in aspect, the younger pale and tense—Rivers began:

"You both know about the job I'm working on. It can be said that you're involved, at least in the fringes of it, and to the extent that you know something of the chief characters concerned."

Truby put in a word at once. "Indeed, yes. Though that applies to me far more than to Peter. I knew Delafield—no matter how slightly—years ago. I went to his house. I met some of his family, and I renewed the acquaintance recently, just before all this trouble began."

"And I also went to the house, and took an interest in the house and its occupants," said Peter.

"Very well. You both know that one of the things which aroused suspicion was the fact that we—the police—have been unable to trace the plasterer who worked in the house. It seemed obvious that this man was an essential witness, but because we could get no exact information about him it was not easy to trace him. The man who was run down this evening was an old man, of working-class type. He lived in a single room behind a second-hand furniture shop near Lisson Grove—less than a mile from the Delafield's house. The owner of the shop says he was a useful 'odd-job man,' an old tradesman who could turn his hand to anything. He had once been in the building trade and sometimes undertook house painting and papering; and he was allowed to borrow his landlord's barrow to move his gear."

"God bless my soul!" exclaimed Mr. Truby. "You think you have found the missing plasterer."

"I don't know," said Rivers. "I only know that the old man is now dying in Paddington Hospital, and that it's not very likely that he will recover consciousness before he dies. But he may; and we have someone sitting by his bed in case he has a lucid moment. Now, this old man was knocked down by a big saloon car which mounted the pavement. The car was described by a constable who saw it pass him as grey or grey-green, and the letters ME or WE were part of its registration." He stopped and turned to Peter Raven. "That is why I am here," he went on, "and you tell me you have mislaid your second ignition key."

Peter said nothing, and Jocelyn burst out: "But this is a shocking story. If Peter's car were used for this purpose, it is tantamount to accusing him of complicity in the crime."

"Leaving the word accusation out of it for the moment, it does seem clear that, if Mr. Raven were not driving his own car, it would have been a smart move on the part of a murderer to use this car for what I believe to be a second murder," said Rivers.

"Yes. I see that all right," said Peter. "Anybody could know that I leave my car standing out there. Anybody could observe that I generally go out to a meal in the evening and am out for an hour or so, if not longer. And I suppose universal ignition keys do exist. Every garage owner possesses something of the kind."

Rivers nodded. "So you'll understand why I'm having your car towed away—it will probably have some evidence on it—even negative evidence. Incidentally, what are the chances that your neighbours would have noticed the car being moved?"

"Not too good," said Peter. "The other side of the way is lock-up garages, and the cars are driven by professional chauffeurs who're out all day. There are two flats beyond mine this side, but the occupants of them wouldn't have seen my car being backed out, it doesn't even pass their windows when I back."

"Nevertheless, it is surprising what people do notice," put in Jocelyn Truby cheerfully. He turned to Rivers with a twinkle. "You said something about myself being involved on the fringes of this case, Chief Inspector, and I agreed that this was true. Since you catechised my young friend here on the manner in which he spent his evening, would it interest you to hear about my own movements during the same hours?"

"By all means," said Rivers cheerfully.

"I had a peculiar, I might say a frustrating evening," said Jocelyn. "I have an old friend who lives in the Brompton Road; he is incapacitated by arthritis but still a very keen chess player. I go and spend an evening with him at intervals and we play a game together. Since he is invalidish, I make a point of getting to him early, by eight o'clock."

As Jocelyn paused here, Rivers put in: "May I ask his name?"

"By all means. Mr. Theodore Willet; he lives in a ground-floor flat at 590B Brompton Road. You will find him at home at any time, for he never goes out. I had my evening meal served early, and I left Portman Square by a Number 30 bus about twenty minutes to eight, and alighted at the stop near the Boltons. I rang Mr. Willet's bell, but got no answer. Assuming that his housekeeper was out for a brief walk, I strolled along the main road for some ten minutes and then returned and rang again, with the same result. I may say that I was somewhat disturbed, but decided to try once again after a short interval."

"Had you made an appointment with Mr. Willet?" asked Rivers.

"No. But I never make an appointment with him. He is always at home; his infirmity makes it impossible for him to go out, and his housekeeper takes her off-duty time at the week-ends, when a deputy takes over. My old friend is too helpless to be left alone," said Mr. Truby. "When my third essay resulted in no response, I am afraid that I rang the bell of another flat—greatly to the annoyance of the tenant. The mystery was explained quite simply. Mr. Willet's electric bell was out of order and the housekeeper had not heard it because it did not ring. Since it was then nearly nine o'clock, I decided it was better not to disturb my old friend, so I left and strolled off towards the bus stop."

Mr. Truby picked up the small canvas which had seemed to cause him so much bewilderment when Rivers came in, and he then went on: "This is a painting executed by my niece, Susan. It was recently exhibited at a show held in this room by courtesy of Mr. Raven. I have bought the canvas, and it occurred to me that I might come here to collect it, and also have a few words with my young friend here concerning this—er—*genre*." He turned the canvas for Rivers's inspection.

"Frankly, Chief Inspector, the work of our younger painters leaves me all at sea."

"Wherein I entirely agree with you," said Rivers. "Have you ever driven a car, Mr. Truby?"

It was then that Peter Raven forgot himself so far as to snort, and Truby turned a reproachful eye on him.

"I was a perfectly efficient driver," said the old man, with dignity. "I have a clean sheet. I never hurt a soul, not even myself. Admittedly, I did not greatly care for motoring and it was a matter of satisfaction to me to give up my car when I retired, two years ago; an economy which cost me not a single regret." He looked at Rivers with his kindly smile. "I don't know if my narrative has assisted you or otherwise, Chief Inspector, but I am happy to know that I have told you my evening's activities in full. At my age, it is markedly distasteful to make a mystery of one's doings."

XIII

I

Lancing had taken over duty at the bedside of William Potts, and a bored constable had retired gratefully to report before going to bed himself. There had been precisely nothing to report, but the police are meticulous in the observance of routine. Potts's bed was at the end of the ward, nearest to the door, for which Lancing was grateful. It meant that he could sit on that side of the bed removed from other patients, and that he got an occasional draught of air when the door swung as the ward sister and other nurses went in and out.

It was terribly difficult not to get sleepy, for the ward was warm and silent and very dimly lighted. Lancing looked down the rows of beds and noticed how they made a pattern, with a long perspective of faintly shining floor down the centre, the only focus of light being the ward sister's table, with its shaded lamp. Sister sat there in her immaculate uniform, the red-lined cape around her shoulders giving her an almost heraldic dignity. Sometimes she got up and went behind the screens round a bed half-way down the ward, where a nurse was busy with a newly-operated case, and Lancing screwed up his face unhappily as the plaints of suffering humanity met his ears. Like any other healthy male, Lancing hated hospitals.

He turned to concentrate on the unconscious face of old Potts. With toothless mouth gaping, the old man breathed stertorously, slowly, jerkily, and Lancing found himself counting the slow breaths. Were they through with their case? he wondered. Had all their suspicions and theorisings been at fault, and was Trimming's death just another "home accident," caused by her being startled at the fall of the plaster which this old man had left unsafe? Lancing didn't believe it, but the warm air of the dimly-lit ward somehow had an oppressive—and depressive—effect; men were dying here, only a few feet away from him, as all men must die eventually. And what did it matter anyway?

Then the ward door swung and a probationer nurse came in, a cup of tea in her hand, and she offered it to Lancing, a smile on her cherry-red lips. He took it and thanked her, grateful in a way he couldn't describe—not for the tea, but because the probationer was young and wholesome and pretty, and very much alive. The smile on her lips and in her eyes was not the professional courtesy of the ward sister, it was the lively smile of a young girl for a man whose aspect pleased her. Lancing smiled back, and because he wanted her to stay a moment, he whispered:

"How do you think he is?"

She stood by the bed and laid her fingers on the stringy putty-coloured wrist of the old man, where knotted blue veins showed like cords sunk between the tendons. Then she only shook her head.

"I don't know. I'll get Sister if you like. She doesn't expect him to live through the night; they generally go out in the early morning—before the day staff comes on."

"Don't bother," said Lancing. "And thanks a lot for the tea. It's so hard not to get sleepy."

"You're telling me," she flashed back, her eyes as merry as a child's.

Just as he put his cup down, Lancing saw the old man move a little; his hand twitched and his head turned a bit on the pillow.

On impulse, Lancing said: "Wally... Walter..." And for a second the lids flickered and the bloodless lips moved. Ward sister was beside him in a moment, with a frown for the young probationer who came back to pick up the teacup.

"It won't be very long now," said the older woman. "Keep your eyes on his face. They sometimes do have a lucid interval just before the end. I doubt if he'll grasp anything you say, but he may wander a little."

For another weary hour Lancing watched and listened to the laboured breathing. Then, when he glanced up, he realised that dawn was showing its first pale light at the long windows, and suddenly, like a miracle, a blackbird called outside, the note sounding clear between the railway noises from the terminus a few hundred yards away. As though the bird song penetrated to his dulled senses, the old man opened his eyes, and Lancing was certain that he was conscious.

Leaning forward, Lancing said: "Hallo, Mr. Potts. You've had an accident, but you're doing fine."

"Eh?" breathed the old man, and the ward sister came hurrying up, swift and silent.

"Do you remember Mr. Delafield?" asked Lancing, and again Potts grunted. "Eh?"

"Mr. Delafield," said Lancing clearly, and Potts echoed the word, unmistakably. "Delafield."

"And Trimming," added Lancing.

He felt both brutal and futile. What could he expect from an old man who was within minutes of death, and what right had he to blunder in on his passing? Then Lancing forgot his own scruples, forgot everything save that old Potts was answering.

"Mean old bastard," said Potts.

"You went there to work for Mr. Delafield and Trimming?" persisted Lancing.

"Bloody old skinflint," said Potts.

If those were not the last words William Potts spoke, they were the last words which were comprehensible. He uttered sounds which neither Lancing nor the ward sister could make anything of, and then the sounds became a confused babbling, and his fingers clawed at the sheets. Sister took one of his hands in her own and held it until the struggle was over, then she turned to Lancing.

"You can go home to bed now, Inspector. There's nothing more for you to do here." Her voice was impersonal, but kindly enough, though Lancing knew that she only wanted to get rid of him.

"Do you think he knew what he was saying, Sister? He did repeat that name—Delafield."

"Yes, I heard him say it; but I don't think you can argue anything from it at all."

Lancing went out into the corridor where he met the pretty probationer.

"Might have been worse, I can get on now," she said. "I've got to do that bed when the night porter's moved him."

"Just one more job," said Lancing. "Thanks for the tea."

"Not a bit. Cheery-bye. A girl gets used to anything," she said in conclusion.

When Lancing got outside into the grey London dawn he drew in a deep breath of the chill air and listened for a moment to the bird song which sounded incredibly across the dreary street. From square and garden and park away to the south the London blackbirds and thrushes were shouting from sooty treetops, and pert busy sparrows hopped around the pavement twittering over straws.

Sleepy, heavy-headed, Lancing tried to determine if his night's vigil had resulted in anything at all. Finally, he made up his mind. A dying man would never have echoed a name that was entirely unknown to him. Potts had said "Delafield" quite clearly, as though it were a name familiar to him.

"And after all, Potts isn't the only one to say that Delafield was a stingy old blighter," thought Lancing. "Did Potts make a mess of that plastering on purpose, because Delafield wouldn't pay a fair price? And if Delafield was as mean as all that, would he have left a loophole for Trimming to feather her own nest? After all, he wasn't senile before his last seizure, he could write cheques and add up, and keep within his income…"

With a huge yawn, Lancing made up his mind that the whole case which he and Rivers had been elaborating was a jumble of unjustified assumptions. The plasterer had fudged his work and Trimming had crashed downstairs when the ceiling fell. And Trimming had been buried and Potts was in the hospital mortuary, and that was that. A night in a hospital ward had blunted Lancing's capacity for original thought.

2

Mr. Truby had used the word "frustrating" to describe his evening; he had probably picked up the word from his young friends, because it was not part of the general vocabulary of his generation. Lancing might well have used it to describe his vigil by the death bed of William Potts, and Rivers refrained from using it by a conscious effort when he got to bed in the small hours.

There was very little chance of checking Mr. Truby's story of his abortive efforts to pay a visit to his old friend. To the indignation of several tenants the electric bell at 590B had been examined at an hour when tenants expect to have peaceful possession of their premises. The bell was out of adjustment and it was a very poor fixture, anyway; it had given trouble before, said the housekeeper. It was also in a position where any enterprising visitor could organise its maladjustment.

Young Raven's car had been towed to the police garage and examined meticulously by a number of people. It showed no sign of any collision; if it had knocked down Mr. Potts, Mr. Potts had failed to leave dent or scratch on the beautiful wings and no tell-tale scrap of fabric was caught in the smooth surface of the bumpers. Indeed, the bumpers seemed to have been specifically designed to avoid catching incriminating particles. The car had been driven by somebody who wore gloves. Wheel, gear lever and door handles yielded no prints save some smudged records of Peter Raven's own fingers. Peter himself did not wear driving-gloves except in midwinter, but that proved nothing.

Mrs. Murphy and two other witnesses of the accident were brought in a police car to identify the suspected vehicle, but their evidence was contradictory. Mrs. Murphy stuck to her previous statement—the car which she had seen was a blue car. As Mrs. Murphy had been stood a variety of drinks while she described her experience in the saloon bar of the King's Head her evidence was not so valuable as it might have been, "and she's probably colour blind, anyway" as one of the police clerks suggested. Rivers, always reasonable, admitted that the grey-green of the car was an elusive colour to recognise in a poor light, and tried to elicit a description of the driver. All witnesses agreed that the driver was "a big chap." "He sat high," said Mrs. Murphy. But Rivers knew that a substantial cushion could add to the appearance of height. He had worn a hat, well pulled down, and glasses, according to one witness. (Peter never wore a hat.) Constable Brown had only witnessed the rear of the car, but gave a firm opinion that this was the car he had seen, and added the sensible comment that the driver was a skilled one. "He could never have got a car that size round the corner at all, not at the speed he was going, if he hadn't been well in control," he said. But he also said that if a driver took that corner at speed he might well have mounted the pavement unintentionally.

Such was the sum total of the evidence offered, but Rivers was not depressed by it. He believed that William Potts had been invited to meet somebody at that particular corner, and told to wait on the kerb ready to be picked up. Regarded in that light, it was a very simple murder.

3

It was shortly after nine o'clock next morning that Rivers rang the bell at another "mews flat." This was on the north side of Regents Park on the verges of Camden Town, a not very attractive neighbourhood in which Susan Truby and her friend Jill Grantham had found a corner to house themselves and their painting gear.

Susan opened the door; she was clad in a painter's smock, well bedaubed with signs of her trade, but she looked as neat as ever, her dark hair and fresh young face making nothing of the stained overall. Rivers had a pang of compunction when he saw the serenity of her eyes displaced by worried apprehension when she saw him. He liked the look of Susan, liked her mannerliness and gaiety, and was genuinely sorry that he had to spoil her day.

"I apologise for coming so early," he said, but she replied:

"It's all right. I'm one of those early risers. Will you come in? I hope you don't mind the stink."

The "studio"—a not very large living-room—reeked of paint and oil and turpentine, and there was a sizable canvas on an easel facing the light. Susan indicated a chair, offered a cigarette, and then said: "What is it?"

Rivers did not beat about the bush, he plunged straight in. "Peter Raven lent you his spare ignition key."

She met his eyes squarely. "Yes; and I've lost it. I'm terribly sorry, but that's how it was."

"You heard that I went to see him last night?"

"Yes. My uncle came on here after he left Peter's. He was terribly worried—Jocelyn, I mean. He was certain I had had the key. Please, can't you tell me if you have found out if it *was* Peter's car that caused the accident?"

"I can't tell you in any case, because I don't know myself," rejoined Rivers. "But I think you'd better tell me about the key."

"It was just as he told you. I've had the key before, because Peter's never quite certain when he can get away from his office, and it's such a bore for him coming right out here to fetch me. So he parks the car somewhere sensible and gives me the spare key, and I get in and wait for him if he's not there first."

"Yes. I see. And what do you do with the key?"

"I put it in my bag and I give it to him when he comes. But last time I forgot to give it back to him."

"Sure?" asked Rivers. He was certain that she wasn't sure, but she replied at once:

"Of course. He asked for it next time he saw me, and I said I was sorry and groped in my bag—and it just wasn't there."

Rivers glanced round the room. There was the inevitable divan, in a gay striped cover, piled with cushions, and against one of the cushions lay Susan's neat leather handbag.

"Do you generally leave it there?" he asked.

She nodded. "I'm afraid I do. It's got my purse in—never with more than a few shillings in, because Jill and I are generally broke, but it's handy to pay the baker and the greengrocer when they come." A sudden smile flashed across her worried face. "We're like Trimming, we pay cash for everything to save having bills. If we had bills, we'd be sunk, but we only buy what we've got pennies to pay for."

"Very sensible. And I wonder how many people have been in this room and noticed that you keep your bag there."

"Almost everybody I know," she said simply. "We can't afford to give parties, not real parties, but we do keep open house, more or less. Our friends just come in and out; and if neither of us is going to be at home when the baker comes, we just leave the key under the mat and the basket inside the door with some money in it, and he leaves the bread and takes the pennies. And we've never lost anything," she added. "It does simplify life when you're not suspicious."

"Yes, it may do, until something goes wrong," said Rivers. "And that's when chaps like me come into the picture and we don't find it simplifies anything."

She took him up at once. "But you don't really like simple explanations, do you?" she asked, her blue eyes challenging him. "You find it easier to believe that people like us—me and poor old Jocelyn and Miss Virgilia and Peter and Roy, and our other friends, are capable of thinking out clever, futile murders. You think we'd push a crazy old woman like Trimming downstairs, and leave Adrian Delafield to die? Why, I don't know, and I don't believe you do, either."

Rivers sat very still. With one side of his mind he thought: "I'm wasting my time; she'll just stick to what she said." But something deeper down gave him a sudden visualisation of Susan strangled with a nylon stocking... Stockings were becoming popular among murderers of a certain type, and once you'd got a nylon stocking pulled tight round a girl's neck there wasn't much she could do about it. So he sat on in his chair, gave her a cigarette, and replied:

"Let's try to sort it out a bit. So far as I can be said to have been trained for anything, I've been trained to look at incidents—violent or accidental death, theft or loss, fraud or blank stupidity—and determine whether the facts merit a detailed and expensive police investigation or not. I've been at it since before you were born. Now I obviously can't tell you all the small things which make me believe that Trimming didn't merely trip over a stair rod, but that she was pushed downstairs with enough violence to kill her. I do believe it. I also believe that an old man named William Potts was knocked down deliberately by a car driven at speed by a very good driver. It was a big car and there is more than a fifty-fifty chance that it was Peter Raven's car. Do you expect me to leave it at that? Do you really want me to leave it at that?"

She flushed, and answered slowly: "When you put it like that, of course there's only one answer. You've got to go on, till you satisfy yourself one way or the other."

"Not myself," said Rivers. "There are more expert minds than mine assessing the evidence, the odd bits and pieces I collect from people like you and your uncle, from Miss Delafield and her nephew—and from Peter Raven. And there's another thing you might bear in mind: once a murderer has got away with it and found it's easy to kill unsuspecting people, he or she will try it again—especially if they think they'd be safer with so-and-so out of the way. And next time it may be you; or more probably your uncle or Miss Delafield, since elderly people are easier to dispose of. Or Peter Raven, since young men who are proud of driving fast can meet something they don't expect to meet. I've quite an open mind."

Her flush had faded now and she looked rather white and sick, but she answered steadily: "Well, what can I do about it?"

"Several things," said Rivers. "You can think over everything you've heard and everything you've said, and let me know if you've anything to add. You can give up your idea of doing a little detecting among the tradespeople Trimming dealt with; and you can give up your habit of leaving the key under the mat. Haven't you any wits?" he cried, allowing his anger to sound in his voice. "Didn't you go out yesterday and leave the key under the mat—and give a chance to whoever wanted it to get that ignition key from your second best bag? Because that bag wasn't the one you had with you when I saw you yesterday. Isn't it because you're proud of not being suspicious that there's no proof that Peter Raven didn't take his car out and knock down an old man in Praed Street?"

"That's not fair!" she cried indignantly. "And nobody with the wits of half a hen would believe Peter murdered anybody, least of all Trimming. Why on earth should he?" She was angry now and went on furiously: "And Jocelyn—just because he got interested in old Adrian Delafield, you think out the chances of his breaking into that house—heaven knows how—and killing Trimming. Or Roy. I suppose he's in it, too, although he was in the south of France when Trimming was killed. Or perhaps you've proved he wasn't there at all."

Rivers's ears, quick to sort out any half-tones, thought: "Hallo… is this what she was leading up to? Peter Raven will have to look out." He answered at once: "I'm pretty certain that Roy Braithwaite was in Arles, as he said he was. He was known by the hotel people there…"

He broke off as Jill Grantham came running into the room.

"Sue, you double-distilled idiot, it's here! It was in the shopping-basket under the potatoes. You must have spilt your whole bag into the basket, because there's your lipstick and our second latch key as well, and my Biro you swore you hadn't touched."

An ignition key lay in the palm of her hand and she tossed it into the air and caught it again. "You'd better jolly well ring up Peter at his office and tell him—and that'll probably be the end of that, for if there's one thing he gets livid over it's anything to do with that ghastly great car."

Rivers was across the room in a trice and he fielded the ignition key as Jill tossed it into the air a second time and she stared at him helplessly.

"Is this assault and battery, or are you the insurance agent?"

"He's Scotland Yard, Jill. Oh, heavens... Chief Inspector Rivers, Miss Grantham."

"Madonna!" exclaimed Miss Grantham inappropriately and went on: "Will it be all right? Does this prove it wasn't Peter's car? Not that I should worry, it may even shatter his superiority a bit—but under the potatoes! I ask you!"

"How long can it have been under the potatoes?" asked Rivers and Susan broke down into helpless laughter—a laughter not far from tears.

"How on earth should I know?" said Jill. "Sue does the shopping and she buys potatoes when she thinks of it. I don't eat them, they're too fattening."

Susan suddenly jumped up and ran out of the room, and Jill said:

"You'd better give it best. It takes her that way when she's upset, and she was terribly upset over Peter being run in or whatever it was."

"He wasn't run in," said Rivers, but she went on:

"Well, Jocelyn seemed to think it was a pretty near thing, and he was all agitated because Peter has been mooching around St. John's Wood. Max saw him there, in a pub." She took a deep breath, and asked: "I feel a bit out of my depth. Peter's brainy and I'm a born fool, so we don't enjoy one another all that. But he was very decent lending his flat for our show, so I hope this clears his character—the ignition key, I mean."

"So do I," said Rivers; "but if you could possibly think out how long the key could have been in the shopping-basket it might help."

"But thinking won't help," she said. "You see, we write shopping lists and put them in the basket and get the shopping and leave the lists in the basket. I'll get it and you'll see."

She ran out and a moment later returned with a basket and a sheet of newspaper, laid the latter on the floor and turned the basket upside down. Some small potatoes, a cloud of dry soil, the outer leaves of some onions and a quantity of old envelopes fell out on to the newspaper.

"It's like that," said Jill. "We're not very methodical in the shopping line, I'm afraid. It might have been there since yesterday or the week before last. I only found it because I knew I'd bought some Kirby-grips and I couldn't find them. You see, one puts one's reticule in the basket and just gropes... or perhaps you don't see."

"Yes, I see," said Rivers resignedly, and Jill began to collect the débris and bundle it up in the newspaper.

"And I should leave Susan alone for a bit," she said. "She doesn't often drop her bundle, but she has this time. After all, one can get upset," she added accusingly.

"Yes. All right," said Rivers. "Just one thing. Will you promise not to leave the latch key under the doormat for the time being—and if that's a duplicate, for goodness' sake put it somewhere sensible and don't leave it kicking around."

"If you say so." She was still kneeling beside the shopping-basket and looked up at Rivers with cheerful inquiry. "You mean we might both be murdered in our beds?"

"Yes," said Rivers. "I do." And he did his best to make his voice convey that he meant it.

XIV

I

WHEN HE LEFT SUSAN'S AND JILL'S FLAT, RIVERS DROVE round the north side of Regents Park and arrived at Firenze in little more than ten minutes. Although the districts were so dissimilar (and many Londoners regard Camden Town as "off the map"), the distance dividing them was quite small. Rivers was more than a bit worried; he felt that the case was in a fluid state and anything might happen. He wasn't at all happy about those two girls, with their haphazard trustful ways, and rather wished he could have found an excuse for "detaining" Susan until he was more certain which way the cat would jump.

Roy Braithwaite admitted Rivers to the studio.

"So things are happening," said Roy. He led the way into the studio where Virgilia was sitting at her desk, a pile of very old papers in front of her.

"Good morning, Chief Inspector," she said, with the calm that never seemed to leave her. "I hope that you will give us an accurate account of what happened in Praed Street last night."

"May I ask how you know that anything happened?" inquired Rivers, after he had returned her greeting.

Roy said flippantly: "Be your age." But Miss Virgilia asked acidly:

"Have you never heard of the Press, Chief Inspector? Freedom of the Press is admirable as an ideal; when it is construed as the right to pester peace-loving writers, I find it less admirable. And, as a source of information, I find reporters most objectionable."

"I'm sorry if you have been pestered," said Rivers; "but you were under no obligation to admit reporters."

"Don't be so high minded," said Roy. "I stayed here with Auntie V. after we saw you yesterday evening, and I'm glad I did. At ten o'clock the bell rang and I found a chap on the doorstep who said: 'I hear the police have found your missing plasterer. Would you care to say a few words?' Well—hell and hades—did you expect me to say, 'Git'? I can assure you I said nothing of the kind. I said, 'Come in and tell us about it,' and he did—with knobs on."

"Spragg," murmured Miss Virgilia, uttering the word with cold distaste. "Albert Edward Spragg. I gather that this person, a vendor of second-hand furniture, entertained the bar parlour nearest to his dwelling with a lively description of a policeman visiting his domicile, and informing him that an old-age pensioner named Potts was the 'plasterer' who repaired my father's drawing-room ceiling. The reporter being present in the same bar, perhaps it was not surprising that he hurried here hoping for some interesting additions to his scoop." She broke off, but before Rivers could get in a word, she added: "You disappoint me, Chief Inspector. You did say that you would let us know if you gained any information on this subject. And this reporter from the local paper was but the harbinger of his colleagues in Fleet Street."

Roy Braithwaite suddenly laughed; his laugh was spontaneous and gay and youthful, and it made Rivers feel old and irritable.

"I was practically chucking them out," he said. "Your chap who was on duty can tell you about it. They were pukka Fleet Street all right, all open and above board, all panting to get headlines about Potts. And who the hell *is* Potts, anyway? It's about time we knew."

"You listen to me," said Rivers, and he said his say for some minutes on end, concluding: "I'm sorry I was unable to come and tell you what had happened, Miss Delafield. I was busy for the greater part of the night trying to find out who was responsible for Potts's death."

"If I was over hasty, Chief Inspector, I beg your pardon," she said. "I admit that I am bitterly disappointed. I had hoped that this distressing muddle was sorted out—as the pressman suggested. It appears that we are only involved in a further, and even more painful, confusion."

"Not of necessity," said Rivers. "It is quite possible that Potts was a one-time employee of your father's. In any case, if he is the man who worked on the ceiling you should be able to identify him. I didn't want to get you out to the hospital last night, and he wasn't really in a state to be identified. I think you'll find it less painful to see him now. I will take you to the mortuary now if you are willing to come."

"Of course I am willing to come," snapped Miss Virgilia. "My one desire is to get the whole mystery cleared up. I only hope with all my heart that my observation of his face will enable me to recognise him—if it indeed be he. I have been looking through this file of old receipts which I found in the studio cupboard hoping that I could find any reference to a workman named Potts, but there's nothing in the least helpful."

2

When they were in the police car—Roy having undertaken to accompany his aunt and add his testimony to hers—Roy asked:

"What's all this huroosh about Peter Raven's car?" Roy and Rivers were sitting in the back of the car and Miss Delafield in front. Rivers had noticed that her face was grey and weary, and, with the consideration he always showed to the elderly, he had put her in front, thinking she would be glad not to have to talk. He turned and looked at Roy, and the latter replied:

"It's not the vine leaf telegraph or secret agents. It's the barber's telephone. You see, I slept on the studio floor last night, to give the aunt a feeling of confidence. I went along to the barber's early to get a shave, as I hadn't any gear with me. While I was there I telephoned to old Truby; Auntie V. asked me to," he added in a lowered voice. "She's agreed at last that she better have a solicitor. She's been amazing, the way she's kept her end up and not got fussed, but she's about at the end of her tether, you know. She's not so young as she was."

Rivers could see Miss Virgilia's profile from where he sat; her eyes were closed and her head nodded with the movement of the car. Seen thus, all her customary vigour seemed to have seeped out of her.

"Poor old girl," said Roy softly. "I wish I could get her right away from that bloody house; she's beginning to look as though she's had it." With a change of tone, he went on: "Truby told me about your visit to Raven's place and all the fuss about his car. It sounds pretty bats to me. Why the hell should Peter get busy knocking out aged plasterers, if that's what the chap was? And as for the thought of old Jocelyn speeding down Praed Street in that outfit—it's the dottiest idea of all."

Rivers was getting a bit tired of the younger generation's derision; he did not answer Roy's comments, but asked:

"Did you ever have a real look at that plasterer's face?"

"No. I saw him once, vaguely; an elderly codger with a shapeless sort of face. I can say what he wasn't like better than what he was like."

3

Rivers stood beside Miss Virgilia in the mortuary and looked down at old Potts. Death had wrought its alchemy on the aged face: the puffiness and skin folds of the living face had been smoothed out, and the dignified mask was subtly different in death. The nose jutted out like a beak, the mouth had fallen in and showed only as a faintly smiling line between unseen lips, the closed eyes were sunk deep under heavy orbital ridges, and the face had been washed clean by a careful nurse—cleaner than it had been since childhood. With smooth white hair and skin the colour of a boiled potato, Potts had a dignity in death surpassing anything he had had in life.

Virgilia Delafield stood and looked at the body in silence. She stood there for quite a long time, and Roy put a hand under her elbow as he saw her sway a little. Then she shook her head helplessly and turned away. Outside, in the grey passage, she faced Rivers.

"I'm sorry, but I can't tell you," she said. "I don't think it can be the man... he had such a foolish face. No. It can't be the same man."

"An old face does alter a great deal after death," said Rivers, and for a moment she recovered her usual acerbity.

"I probably know more about that than you do," she retorted. "So far as I can judge, I have never seen that old man before."

Rivers turned to Roy, who said simply: "I think it's the same chap. Of course he looks different—his nose was a bit red and swollen when I saw him—but I think he's the same." He turned and glanced at his aunt and then jerked his head at Rivers. "Can we get on home. I think it's time."

Miss Virgilia straightened her shoulders and walked steadily towards the car, but her face was nearly as pallid as the face on the mortuary slab.

4

When Rivers had left the studio and taken Miss Virgilia and her nephew to the mortuary, two C.I.D. men entered the studio, using the spare key which Virgilia had given to Rivers. They produced their outfit for bringing up fingerprints, a camera, and a neat bag of tools. They took no notice at all of the pictures (which elicited an exclamation from all but the most hard-boiled), but proceeded at once to the glass-fronted case which held Adrian Delafield's "Alexandra" palette and brushes. This they sprayed with powder, blew off the excess and took photographs of the smudgy result.

"Not been touched in years," volunteered Bob, the older man. Jack, the younger, nodded. He was examining screws, hinges and putty.

"All of twenty years, if not more," agreed Jack. "These screws are going to be a teaser."

They produced an oil can and began to pump in tiny jets of oil on to screw heads and hinges and woodwork. Then they waited a little, and for the first time considered the pictures.

"Very nice," said Bob, and Jack nodded. "That's good work, that is," he agreed. Then they returned to the case. With their outfit of cunning tools, plus skill and a lot of muscular effort, the screws were slowly turned. A fractional turn, then more oil, and so they continued until eight screws were removed undamaged and laid in a row below the case. And then the glass front of its mouldings was opened with a squeak of old hinges, and the palette and brushes were bared for their inspection.

"All of twenty-five years," grunted Bill. "That's good joiner's work; air-tight, I reckon."

They sprayed the palette with powder and photographed it in its place. With gloved hands, as reverently as one handling a relic, Jack lifted down both palette and brushes, and these in their turn were sprayed and photographed from all angles. The palette seemed to be of cedarwood, and its rear surface was smooth and untouched with paint. At the conclusion of the photography, Bob drew a lens from his pocket, fitted it to his eye and scrutinised some of the prints to which the powder adhered on the back of the palette.

"Twenty-five years or not, reckon they're what's wanted," he said. "The old codger made these all right, or I'm a Chinaman. Whorl and loop, same as the sample. O.K."

They dusted their powder off the palette and brushes, replaced them in the case, and screwed the latter up with the same unhurried skill with which they had opened it. Oil was carefully removed and a modicum of dust blown over the surface of the wood.

By the time they had finished their job no ordinary observer could have told that the case had ever been touched, or that any workmen had visited the studio.

5

Lancing had spent an industrious, if unprofitable morning. He had gone through old Potts's humble possessions without finding anything that linked the dead man with the Delafield case—unless an outfit of plasterer's trowels and board could be said to constitute a clue. He learnt that Potts had lived in his present abode for five years, that he had been "bombed out" by a VI, and had lived somewhere in south London for the intervening years. Like many such old men, he took an interest in the pools and the dogs, and he frequently made optimistic forecasts of winnings which were coming his way to-morrow. As to whether Potts had been seen going out to a job on the days which interested Lancing, evidence was so contradictory that it was valueless. If Potts *had* worked at Firenze, he had pushed a barrow there on the Friday, 26th March—over a fortnight ago; and no reliable witness could be found who would swear to it that they had seen the old man push a barrow out of Spragg's yard and turn northwards towards St. John's Wood. Neither had any habitué of Potts's chosen local ever heard him mention the name Delafield. When Potts did get chatty, which was seldom, his chosen topics were the pools and the dogs.

"What did he generally do with himself?" Lancing asked Spragg.

"Well, if I'd told him there was a job for him he'd come in and do it; if not, he'd mooch about like these old chaps do—go and sit on a chair in the park if the sun shone, and then come home with his fish and chips. Or on a wet day he'd go and look at the papers in the public library."

By the time Lancing got back to the Yard, he was beginning to wish he'd never heard of William Potts, and he ate a large meal at the canteen and did *The Times* crossword, hoping for a word from Rivers.

It was two o'clock when Lancing got a message from Rivers. The latter was in his own office, with coffee and sandwiches in front of him and a sheaf of notes which he was endeavouring to make less illegible—they were in his own writing. He glanced up at Lancing, put his notes down, and said:

"This seems to be the lid; a few screws to fasten it down and the case can be buried. All our brighter variations are bust."

"Delighted to hear it," said Lancing. "How and why?"

"Henry Fearon. He rang me from Paris half an hour ago. Cutting out all his cackle about procedure and international monetary dealings, the plain fact is that Delafield did win a pot of money in 1926—not so much as Truby thought, but a nice little packet—and he invested it in France. All shipshape and Bristol fashion. In 1939, sensing that war was likely, he realised his holdings and bunged the capital in deposit in a French bank, with instructions to his bank manager to hold it and add any interest to the principal, pending further instructions. There's a lot of guff about capital losses during the war, but Delafield was informed of the state of his account in 1946, when things had been sorted out, and a letter was received by the French bank instructing them to hold the capital as before. And it's still there, millions of francs, a comfortable little fortune even when translated into sterling. That's the gist of it. Nothing phoney, merely the obstinacy of an old man who swore he wouldn't bring capital to England to have the deposit interest mulcted by the chancellor. And so Trimming never pinched a fortune at all, and Truby never got within the smell of one, and so far as I can see there was no object in anybody killing Trimming—and there you have it."

"Well, well," said Lancing. "That certainly puts paid to some of our notions. Unless there was a will, leaving everything to Trimming," he added as an afterthought.

"Unless. Then why wasn't old Delafield killed too? Kindly remember he was left alive, presumably in bed, and it was only chance he got stuck on the stairs. He might have stayed in bed, alive if not kicking, to make another will another day."

Again Lancing pondered. "Did they identify Potts?" he asked.

"Potts," mused Rivers. "The chap who snaffled Trimming's ill-gotten hoard. You didn't find any of it, did you? No. I didn't think you would. Potts looked like a plaster saint, all washed and purified. Miss Virgilia said she'd never seen him. Roy Braithwaite said, 'Yes, that's the chap.' So you can pay your money and take your choice. Where do we go from now?"

"What you want is a drink. You're in the same state of mind I was in when I came out of that blighted hospital. Did anybody get a line on Peter Raven yesterday evening?"

"Yes. He was seen in the Cumberland at seven-twenty."

"Less than a mile from Praed Street," said Lancing, and Rivers nodded.

"Yes. And his car wasn't in its usual place at seven-fifteen; but nobody saw who moved it. So he could have killed Potts, for all the evidence we have to the contrary. So could Truby, if he's put in a little driving practice recently. He drove a car for twenty years and never had a summons. But why should he have killed Potts? There was no loot for him to snaffle. Oh, a final contribution: Bob and Jack opened up that case with old Delafield's palette in it while we were at the mortuary. They say it hadn't been opened for years—screws rusted right in. There were some excellent prints on both palette and brushes—Delafield's. The old chap in St. John's Hospital—our old chap—is the same one who left his dabs on the palette and brushes after he painted Alexandra. So Trimming never did the famous transformation act after all."

Lancing began to laugh. "It's a glorious clean sweep, Julian. All the same the transformation possibility *was* pointed out by old Truby."

"It jumped to the eye. We both pondered over it," said Rivers disgustedly.

"And barring the chance of that palette having Delafield's dabs on it, we should still be pondering," said Lancing.

Rivers nodded. "It was Miss Virgilia put that one into my head," he said. "She told me how he had put the palette there 'with his own hands.'"

Again they sat in silence for a moment. Then Lancing said: "Anything further about Roy being seen in France?"

"Yes. He was there all right—no possibility of his having been over here. He wants to get his aunt away from the studio, and I can't blame him. She's showing signs of wear; her only cheerful remark was that her father's quite comfortable and may live for some time. Why she should be glad of that, I can't imagine. He's only a living corpse. She's gone to the hospital to sit with him, and Roy's started taking down the pictures in the studio."

"What have you done about Raven's car?"

"Let him have it back. There was no evidence."

"No," said Lancing slowly. "And among all this welter of above-boardiness, we still haven't any reasonable explanation of why Raven has been seen mooching round this district. He has, you know."

"Yes. So I'm told. And he has no real alibi for last night—no one saw him go into that cinema—and he says he was at home, reading, when Trimming fell downstairs. But where he comes in—G.O.K."

Rivers went and stood looking out at the river, far away below, and Lancing turned over Rivers's notes of Henry Fearon's telephoned report. Then Rivers said slowly:

"I wonder..."

Lancing pricked his ears up, but Rivers only said:

"Bright idea the last; final instalment. Nothing for you to do. Another of those routine jobs for the experts."

"O.K.," said Lancing. "If you don't want me to pick any more rags in Lisson Grove, I'll go and see a man about a dog. He's a chap who was in Field Security with Peter Raven, and he happens to be arriving on leave to-day."

"O.K. by me," said Rivers, "though if my final idea's right, yours will probably be wrong—unless, of course… oh, well, never mind."

"Go and get outside that drink," said Lancing. "You need it."

XV

I

RIVERS FELT BETTER AFTER HE HAD DONE HIS LARGE GROUSE to Lancing. One of the pleasant things about his association with Lancing was that he could blow off steam to him—Lancing never let him down. Rivers went out and got his drink and then came back to write up a comprehensive report, including Henry Fearon's evidence, to put before the Commissioner. It was up to that eminent official to decide if further investigation was justified in a case which gave negative reactions to all suspicions. But even as he wrote, Rivers's natural obstinacy reasserted itself; he had believed that Trimming was thrown downstairs, and he still believed it. He believed that old Potts had been run down deliberately, to provide an explanation of the missing plasterer, and he still believed it. As he got his report into order, Rivers was rather glad that his "final idea" could not be incorporated into it, whether the idea was proved fallacious or not. It would take time to get the evidence he wanted, he knew that.

Finally, he began to think about the Delafield's house again. He had been all over it, from attics to cellar, and he visualised it as he sat at his desk and then said to himself: "Lancing and I will go over it again to-morrow, every bit of it, and over the garden, too. If we don't spot anything, I'll hand it back to Miss Virgilia and leave her to it. I think it's about time she moved away from that studio."

It was when he had arrived at this conclusion, and the sheets of his report were ready for the typist, that his telephone rang.

The switchboard operator told him that a Miss Susan Truby was asking to speak to him. Rivers's mind gave a jump. "Hallo, has she decided to come across with something?" he hazarded, and glanced at his clock; it was close on six o'clock. He had put in nearly four hours over his report and his final "think"—and he hadn't given a thought to Susan for hours.

"Put her through," he said.

"Chief Inspector Rivers? It's Susan Truby. I'm terribly sorry to bother you, but I'm worried stiff. It's about Peter."

Rivers nearly said, "Damn Peter," but he only uttered an interrogative "Yes?"

"He rang up at lunch and asked me to meet him at five o'clock," she said. "He said he'd arranged to get away early and would I meet him at the Piccadilly end of Berkeley Street. I've been here nearly an hour and he hasn't come. I rang his office and he left there at five, in his car."

Rivers heard her draw a long breath, quite audible on the telephone, and then she rushed on: "I'm sorry if I'm just being silly, but I remember what you said this morning, and he does drive fast. Can you find out—if anything's happened?"

"I'll try," said Rivers. "Where are you now?"

"In a telephone kiosk in Berkeley Street. The only thing I could think of was to let you know."

"Well, say if you go home and stay there," said Rivers. "Go by bus and don't do anything idiotic. Is Miss Grantham there?"

"Yes. She's got a woman model she's painting."

"All right. Go home and paint the model, too."

"You'll let me know if you... find anything?"

"Yes. Look here, have you any private reason for thinking that Raven was butting into something on his own?"

"I know he'd got an idea, but he wouldn't talk about it," said Susan. "He's been queer ever since this horrible business started."

"And you can't tell me what his idea is?"

"No. Honestly I can't. He hasn't told me a thing."

"All right. I'll get going and see if we can trace him. And you're to go home and stay there. Got that?"

"Yes. I'll go; by bus; all the way."

2

Rivers rang down to the Mobile Police department.

"I put in an instruction about a grey Lee-Jaegar, XME 9807. Check up on it. I'm just coming down."

Without the least conviction that it would lead to anything, after the car had been returned to Peter's address, Rivers had issued an order to police patrol cars to keep an eye open for XME, and be prepared to report its direction if asked; and despite his assertion about "screwing his case down" he had not cancelled the order. Wherever a radio-equipped police patrol-car saw XME, a report on its position would be radioed to the panel at Scotland Yard.

Rivers went along to the radio room, where operators sat with headphones on, talking their own variety of jargon. There was a chase in progress at the moment. A doctor's car had been stolen from outside the practitioner's house while the latter was snatching a cup of tea, and the Flying Squad was hot on the trail. One of the operators glanced at Rivers as he came in and held out a note block to him without stopping his monotonous murmur:

"C.O. Control Room to Squad car T for Tommy. Message received. Blue Austin MBY 8096 reported in Church Street, Kensington, heading south. Over..."

Rivers perched on a stool and studied the note block.

"10.30 a.m. Lee jaegar XME 9807 parked in Summer's Walk, S.W.10.

"1.45 p.m. XME 9807 collected by owner (P.S.W. Raven).

"1.55 p.m. XME 9807 parked by Horse Guards.

"4.58 p.m. XME 9807 reversed at Marlborough Gate causing obstruction and near collision, reported by Traffic Police. Then headed east to Admiralty Arch.

"5.10 p.m. XME 9807 reported in St. Martin's Lane, heading north. Identity uncertain but probable.

"5.20 p.m. XME 9807 reported heading east High Holborn.

"5.30 p.m. XME 9807 reported Chancery Lane, heading south."

The operator who had handed Rivers the note block was talking again into his mouthpiece, still in the same unanimated professional monotone.

"Blue Austin, MBY 8096 brought to a standstill outside Olympia by traffic block. Driver alighted, being followed by Constable Newton. Your message received by C.O. O.K. Over."

The operator turned to Rivers with a grin. "Nice work. Got him in under the hour. Now, about yours, sir."

"Yes, about mine. He's either doing a bolt or chasing someone else—or else he's gone mad."

"He's chasing another car, sir. Welcome there has got some more gen for you."

Another note block was shoved into Rivers's hands, and he read:

"XME 9807 reported to be following an open sports model, BYU???? Last seen in Strand, heading west."

"You didn't say you wanted him pulled in, sir; just reported," said Welcome firmly.

"Yes. O.K. I'll ring down for a squad car and join in. He must be up to something. Good work, you chaps. But if he's chasing a small sports car, why hasn't he caught up? He's a good driver and those Lee Jaegars can jump to it."

"They're too big, sir," said Welcome. "The little ones can beat them in traffic—get in and out like a taxi. On the open road it'd be a different story... C.O. here; message received. XME 9807 reported Piccadilly, heading west... Hold on..."

"Do you want him stopped, sir? They can get him at any of the traffic lights."

"No. I'm going myself. Report that I shall keep in touch from squad car. No poaching. Warn all units we're following," said Rivers.

He was out of the room and on the stairs in a trice, thankful for the chance of action. As he bundled into the Flying Squad car, Rivers felt as though he'd been sitting still chewing over possibilities—and impossibilities—like a dog with a dry bone. Now he was going to crack the bone—with luck.

"If the big fool was on to something, why didn't he tell us?" he thought, as they slid out of the gates at Cannon Row and cut across the traffic, police lights up, gong sounding.

"Unless he was responsible for the whole shemozzle—and if so, the deuce alone knows why, because I don't. There's nothing in it for anybody," thought Rivers disgustedly.

The radio operator in the back of the car was doing his stuff. Another squad car had joined in the chase ahead, discreetly, observing the "no poaching" order. The Lee Jaegar had reached the traffic lights at Hyde Park Corner by the time Rivers's car turned into Constitution Hill, but the system of police-box phones and walkie-talkie operators had gone into action, and they raced across the streets with every traffic policeman working like a hero to give them a clear passage. They cut across prohibited lanes at Hyde Park Corner like royalty, and swung westwards by St. George's Hospital when XME was passing the end of Sloane Street.

It was in the congested traffic by South Kensington Station that they first caught sight of the grey-green Lee Jaegar, with Peter Raven's bare dark head unmistakable above the wheel. By that time, their police notice had been lowered and they were driving as sedately as the speed of the Lee Jaegar ahead permitted them to do, the object being to keep it in sight—and themselves out of sight.

"He's a damn' good driver, I'll say that for him," said Hilton, Rivers's driver (a handsome tribute coming from one of the best drivers in the Flying Squad); "but if he thinks he's going to beat it, doesn't he know we could have picked him up anywhere we wanted since he started goating about?"

"I don't think he's bothering about us," rejoined Rivers. "He's got a private game of his own on, and neither he nor the sports car wants to attract attention; they haven't jumped the lights or done anything they could be stopped for. The only chance this bloke took was when he turned right-about in the Mall, and my bet is that he saw someone he wanted and has stuck to his tail ever since."

"Know who he's after, sir?"

"Search me," said Rivers.

They turned into Brompton Road and Rivers had a wild idea that Peter Raven was going to foregather with Mr. Truby's aged friend, but they went steadily on down the long dull road which ran south-westwards and changed its name at intervals: the Old Brompton Road became Richmond Road and Richmond Road became Lillie Road.

"We shall get to the river soon," observed Hilton dispassionately, "unless he takes the Fulham Palace Road, and if he does that—well, we've got all England to choose from. No. He's going over—Crabtree Lane, isn't it? There's some wharves and shacks ahead."

They crossed the Fulham Palace Road and soon were in much narrower streets, playing hide-and-seek now, spinning round corners on roads never meant for fast traffic or big cars.

"I hope to God he doesn't kill some of those kids," said Hilton, for children were swarming over the pavement. "Cripes, he's had it. No, he hasn't—but we have."

A van had slewed round a blind corner, and the big Lee Jaegar pulled in, then mounted the pavement and somehow got by, while the van driver swore bitterly and halted his vehicle right across their way.

"Put a sock in it, mate," said Hilton, "and back there. Back, you great…"

The police sign shot up again and the van backed slowly, but by the time they had negotiated the next corner there was no sign of either the Lee Jaegar or the sports car. It was then that a small cockney—a filthy lively-looking brat armed with a toy pistol—yelled to them. "They've gorn down to Crabtree Wharf, mister; down there. I'll show yer, 'ere give me a lift and I'll show yer."

"No, you won't, thanks all the same," said Hilton, as he put a hand out of the window and shoved the brat off. "That's torn it," he added, for all the young desperadoes of the pavements took it into their heads to hold up the police car by crowding solidly across the road—knowing perfectly well that no police driver would run them down. By the time they had turned the corner, the Lee Jaegar had disappeared again. It was Rivers who spotted it, pulled up in a dead end which apparently led to nothing but a big gate, closed in front of one of the yards connected with the wharves. Of the sports car there was no sign.

"All right, drop me here. I'll whistle if I want you," said Rivers. "They can't be far away."

3

There was, as Rivers guessed, a footpath leading from the cul-de-sac; he glanced down it, but there was nobody there. Then he put his shoulder to the big gate and found it gave a little; another shove and he could see through into the yard, where the sports car stood. Obviously enough the yard gates had been open and the small car driven straight in; then the gates had been shoved to—but there was no sign of either driver. Rivers looked at the big doors of the "Furniture Depository"—its description was painted on a board above the door, together with the name of the owner. He was just going to try the door when something—perhaps a sound, perhaps instinct—made him look back through the partially open gates through which he had come. A man in workman's clothes was slouching towards the corner—a commonplace figure in a drab raincoat and cloth cap with a scarf round his neck. Rivers shouted:

"Hi, there! Wait a minute."

The man walked on, and Rivers suddenly started in pursuit—for no reason at all except that the man had not stopped. At the sound of the gate creaking open, the other stopped and looked round.

"What yer doing there?" he demanded and took a step towards Rivers—who knew that he had never seen this man in his life.

"I'm looking for the drivers of those two cars," he said.

"Them? Oh, they've gone into the shack round the corner; they're artists or something." Suspicion is second nature to a

C.I.D. man. Rivers sensed that the rough voice, speaking with a cockney accent, was bogus. It wasn't really a cockney voice. How his suspicion conveyed itself to the other he did not know, but in a flash the fellow was on him—not at his throat, but at his knees, a rugger tackle, with all the other's weight and spring behind it, flinging Rivers off his feet so that he went down backwards, carried back by the other's impetus. Rivers fell flat, but at least he knew how to fall. He was not knocked out, and snatched at his whistle even as he fell, and he heard the sound of the whistle at the same time that he heard the other's running footsteps.

The man ran fast, head down, all out—too fast to pull up in the split second he needed, for Hilton had moved the police car forward to block the entrance to the cul-de-sac. It was hardly a matter of the car knocking the fugitive down; the latter hit the moving bonnet, hit the wings and bumpers and went down with a thud, while the well-trained Hilton stepped on the brake before the wheels even touched the fallen man. But the force with which he fell knocked the senses out of him and he lay like a log, hard up against the tyres of the police car.

Rivers had got to his feet in time to see what happened. The radio operator was out of the car by this time, and Rivers said: "Handcuff him and shove him in the back and stay there with him. Come on, Hilton, the other bloke's about somewhere—and if he's alive, he's lucky."

They ran down the cul-de-sac and turned into the alleyway; it led only to another block of buildings; there were two doors and one of them had a well-painted sign above it: "De Fraine. Frescoes and Tempera." Rivers gave one brief exclamation, "Frescoes... hell," before he put his shoulder to the door. It was locked, but Hilton pulled a tool out of his pocket without a word. It might have been a tyre-lever; it might have been one of those tools which a man can be arrested for carrying, but in Hilton's hands it made short work of a not-very-powerful lock. The door gave, and the two C.I.D. men went cautiously forward into a long room, grey in the fading light. The walls were covered with paintings, but a heap of curtains or drapery lay on the ground. It was a very long heap and Rivers pulled them up knowing what he would find. Peter Raven lay there on his face, looking even longer than usual stretched out on the floor. Rivers bent over him, felt a pulse and heard him breathe, and said:

"Well, he's alive. Whether he deserves to be is a different matter." He got up, adding: "Here's someone else, coming to join the party."

"Hands up there," said a crisp voice. The light was very dim in the long studio, and perhaps Lancing could not have been blamed for not recognising his superior officer, but he didn't take long.

"You've beaten me to it!" he exclaimed.

"Raven acted as unintentional guide," said Rivers. "Help me to heave him over. Our bloke ought to have called up an ambulance by now. What do you know about all this?" he demanded of Lancing.

"Not much. De Fraine, the tenant of this place, was in the army with Raven and Braithwaite. When I heard he was a swell at fresco painting, I thought I'd come along and have a look. They lay the plaster first and put the tempera on wet, don't they? Anyway, they lay the plaster."

"Perfectly true," said Rivers. "Odd how miscellaneous information comes in useful to a policeman. Presumably we've got the missing plasterer in the back of our car. He obliged by hitting it."

"And who hit this one?" asked Lancing.

"Presumably the plasterer," said Rivers. "This is where we think things out afresh."

The ambulance came up and two unconscious forms were strapped to stretchers and loaded up. Then Rivers and Lancing searched the old house where De Fraine, fresco painter, occupied the big ground-floor room only. They saw some very good frescoes, and a nice demonstration of the method, where one wall had been relaid with enough wet plaster to occupy the painter during his chosen working hours. They found all the tools of a plasterer's trade and an interesting collection of tempera colours and mediums. But they found nothing to connect De Fraine with the Delafield case.

It was late when Rivers got home, and as he headed for the bathroom he suddenly said: "Damn." He had forgotten all about Susan Truby. He went to the telephone and rang her number.

"Miss Truby?... Rivers here. We found Raven. He got knocked down and we've sent him to hospital... No. I don't think he's badly hurt, just concussed a bit. Good night."

He rang off before Susan had time to thank him. He didn't very much want to be thanked—by Susan.

XVI

I

IT WAS RIVERS WHO ARRIVED FIRST AT FIRENZE THE FOLLOWing morning. He let himself in at the front door with the latch key which had once been carried by Trimming, and stood in the gloomy hall, sensing the stale dank atmosphere of the shut-up house. Dust lay thick everywhere—plaster dust. It had seeped through from the drawing-room, blown by the draught from the boarded-up windows; it outlined the geometrical pattern of the hideous tiled floor, and it lay thickly over the dried dribbles of milk and the smear of fat left when the supper tray had been tumbled downstairs; and still showing amid the dust, a whiter line chalked by the careful Dowding showed how Trimming had lain, a black form on a dusty floor.

Rivers was inured to the depressing qualities of a house where murder had been committed; he had been in many such houses, kept vacant by the police during their investigation, but he found some particularly dreary quality in the dated dignity of Firenze because the squalor of neglect seemed so foreign to it. He was standing at the drawing-room door, looking at the broken clock which had roused his suspicions, when Lancing turned up.

"Hallo. Any chirp and chat from the pair of charmers we sent to hospital yesterday?" asked Lancing.

"Nothing. Raven is still unconscious, he was efficiently coshed from the rear, and it may be some time before he can give his version. De Fraine was conscious, but very sick and sorry for himself and has obliged with nothing but groans," said Rivers. "And Henry Fearon has beaten us to it again," he added. "I had a perfectly good idea, though I admit it was a delayed action one, and I got all the best chaps cracking at Somerset House, only I didn't know anything about the date concerned, and searching's a slow business."

Lancing stood still and stared. "Somerset House?" he queried, and Rivers watched his face.

"The day's great thought," he said flippantly. "Got it? He married her. Adrian Delafield married Trimming in August 1939. And kept quiet about it. As for Trimming, I suppose she was cranky enough to hug her secret and feel her power. As Roy Braithwaite says, 'She was a secret sort of person.' Well, now we know."

"Has Fearon found a will?"

"No, and I shouldn't think he's likely to. Delafield probably wrote one on half a sheet of notepaper, because he was too mean to pay a solicitor, and it's been destroyed, together with a number of other items. But even if Delafield had died intestate, his widow would have got a very nice rake-off."

"So that was it," said Lancing slowly. "It's an illuminating thought. Well, I suppose the problem is still the same. How did anybody get out of this house after shoving Trimming—I beg her pardon, Mrs. Delafield—downstairs?"

"That's where we think again," said Rivers. "This house is as it was when Longaby broke in. We have had the window boarded up and we have come in and out by the front door, but everything that was locked and chained when he came in is still locked and chained. We'd better find the answer—because there must be one."

"Well, I vote for further consideration of the bedroom window."

"It won't do. Delafield was left alive. It was natural causes that determined his seizure, and he wasn't deaf. No one could have gone through his bedroom, opened that window, and shut it again behind them without waking him. If that window had anything to do with it, it'd have been the easiest thing in the world to tip the old man downstairs too. And every other window in the place is still latched and most of them stuck tight in addition. Like the case which holds the palette, they are evidence in themselves."

They went round the house again, testing bars and bolts and locks; they examined the coal cellar hatch, the trapdoor to the roof—all the odd exits which criminals sometimes use. And at last, defeated, they stood again by the fake-antique door which gave on the covered way. It also was bolted, and a heavy chain was securely in its place. Rivers stood and stared at it, and as he did so Lancing swung the clapper of the cracked bell, and its ominous note set the air aquiver.

"I hate the thing," said Rivers. He unhitched the chain and shot back the bolt and then produced the unwieldy key which Virgilia Delafield had given him and put it in the lock and shot the wards back. They were noisy, and he remembered how Dr. Longaby had said he heard the wards shoot back before Virgilia Delafield had shaken the door—and how he himself had shaken it, too, and known it was bolted on the inside. Standing very still, Rivers suddenly muttered an oath and Lancing stared at him—Rivers was seldom profane. Then holding the key with both hands he turned it, and turned it again twice round.

"It's a double lock," he said. "Some old locks are like that. You turn the key twice on the outside and then the door can't be opened from the inside. She double-locked it outside and only turned the key back once for Longaby's benefit, so of course he thought it was bolted—and she would have shot the bolt while he was bending over the body and put the chain up when he went outside to telephone. It was as easy as that."

2

Turning the big key again, twice round, Rivers set the door open, and the April sunshine reflected back into the gloomy hall. He was just going to fit the key into the outside of the door when he saw that Virgilia Delafield was standing in the covered way, close to the door.

"I heard the bell," she said. "I once called it the crack of doom; and I heard you turn the key, twice. It took you a long time to think it out, didn't it? I have often noticed that people with the ablest minds are slow to realise very simple things."

Her voice was perfectly steady, her face the colour of old parchment, but she stood firmly, very still.

"I killed Trimming—of course," she said, almost scornfully, and Rivers jerked himself back to reality to speak the oft-repeated words of caution which his duty impelled him to speak.

"That is redundant," she said coldly. "I am perfectly prepared to tell you anything you haven't realised for yourself; and let me tell it here. I find it a fitting place."

There was a frigid dignity about her which impelled compliance, and Rivers stood perfectly still and let her have her say, standing in the sunshine which gleamed across the covered way.

"I came into this house and stood on the landing in the dark," she said. "Trimming would never turn the gas up—she was mean all through. If you want to know, I used a well-padded broom—and pushed hard. I am still very strong, and it worked. It was the crash of her fall which brought the ceiling down—that had all been arranged for—it seemed a very simple and obvious accident."

A queer contraction crossed her ashen face. "I would do it again; I hated her," she said tensely. "You know my father married her? She was to have everything at his death—everything. And when she realised that I knew about this preposterous marriage, she taunted me." Her breath was coming quickly now, but she still had herself under control. "Will you come to the studio?" she said. "There is something there that you should see—before you take me away. I will come quietly, as your jargon has it. Believe me, I am very tired. But if Trimming were still alive, I would kill her again, with my own hands."

She turned resolutely, towards the house, and Rivers walked on one side of her, Lancing on the other, for there was something about Virgilia Delafield which made Rivers want to accede to the last request which would ever be granted to her as a free woman. And he now had a grim premonition of what he was to see.

3

At the far end of the studio, on an improvised bed on the floor, Roy Braithwaite lay like one sleeping, but his sleep was the sleep of death.

Virgilia stood and looked down at him. "He was my son," she said simply. "Mifanwy took him after he was born and brought him up as her own. It was harder for unmarried mothers in those days, and I lost my job and I was very poor. I asked my father for money, telling him I was ill, and he refused to help. Trimming poisoned his mind—she would not let him help. I never forgave them—neither of them. He could have helped so easily—he had just won that lottery you talked such a lot about. But no; everything was to go to Trimming. Perhaps the seeds of all this evil were planted then, when I was penniless and in disgrace, and I let my baby go. It was better for him, and Mifanwy cared for him as her own, though she was poor, too—and my father was rich and would not help." She looked down broodingly at the body on the floor. "It's better so," she said. "I killed Trimming, and I would do it again. But our plan encompassed only Trimming's death, and I was prepared to take the responsibility for that if need arose. But Roy—he was of his generation; he had to be clever. He could not leave a simple idea alone."

One part of Rivers's mind was shaken with horror—and pity. Something about the stoic calm of the grey-haired, ashen-faced woman moved him intensely, but controlling that errant sense of humanity was the detective's desire for evidence, and something told him that after this impulse to speak was exhausted, Virgilia Delafield would never speak again.

"It was Roy who thought out the business of the plasterer and got one of his friends to work on the ceiling?" he asked.

"He would have it that way," she said slowly. "I told my father I had ordered the man to come, and he accepted it. You see, I was winning back some influence over him, and Trimming did not always win—not over small things—she knew she had won what she wanted. I agreed with Roy's plan, on condition that he should be in France. I alone was to take responsibility for what I did. But he could not leave well alone. He killed that silly old man—Potts. Potts had worked here many times and Roy used him as an explanation." Still with that brooding look of pity, with her eyes on the body at her feet, she went on: "He should not have done that; it was evil—and silly. I knew you would find out—about Potts." The ghost of a faint smile twitched her blue lips. "I had not envisaged an investigator such as you; some foolish policeman, perhaps, to write down details of an accident—and Dr. Longaby is a dull fellow. One makes these mistakes."

"You killed your son?" said Rivers, and she nodded.

"It was better so—better than letting him live to be hanged, as you would have hanged him. It was very easy. When he was in Germany, he obtained some of those poison capsules we heard so much about when the Nazis were taken. He left them with me, so that I could take my own way out if things went awry. I could have left a confession, and Roy would have been quite safe. But he had to interfere, to bring in his friends to complicate the issue—that silly old man, and the tall boy who was not so silly." Again she looked at Rivers, with that faint suggestion of a twisted smile. "I think you understand it all now—you have a not insensitive mind, Chief Inspector. And this is the end. All you need now is the mortuary van."

Suddenly she went down on her knees beside the body, and Rivers did not move. He knew what was coming, for every policeman knew about the Nazi poison capsules. Whatever his sense of duty, he was not prepared to grapple with the greyfaced woman in a futile attempt to keep her alive and bring her to justice.

4

A few minutes later Rivers and Lancing went into the sunny garden. Virgilia Delafield's last words were true, and they had ordered the mortuary van. Round the Florentine well-head the daffodils were fading now, and rank grasses and weeds were growing over the drooping flowers. Rivers pulled out his cigarette case, and they lighted up, and Lancing said:

"I was never so completely shattered in my life. I thought there was a fifty-fifty chance she did it, but I didn't guess the background story."

"I wondered," said Rivers. "Roy was ten years younger than his brother, and ten years is quite a gap; but Virgilia played the part of maiden aunt so perfectly she'd have fooled anybody. And until this morning I could not see how she had got out of the house; but the problem of inheritance complicated things to start with. There was the insistence at the outset that old Delafield had nothing but his annuity; then the denial of Truby's story about the lottery. The accent was all on nothing left to inherit, but when Truby put in his quite ingenious suggestion that Trimming had provided a substitute for Adrian Delafield, Miss Virgilia was furious. She—and Roy—intended to make it quite clear that the old chap *was* Delafield; and Miss Virgilia indicated the case with the palette in most skilfully. She did not say in so many words 'Open that case. His fingerprints must still be on it.' She said, 'He put the palette and brushes there with his own hands,' and left me to take the implication."

"So you knew that she wanted to establish the fact that the old man *was* Delafield," said Lancing, "and that made you think of the inheritance theme again."

"Or thinking of the inheritance theme made my subconscious mind get busy on those who might inherit," said Rivers. "I think it's true that one's mind works on different levels, and sometimes ideas come popping up from underneath somewhere. It was probably because I pondered over the inheritance theme that I found myself asking, 'Did Delafield marry Trimming?' If he did, she was due for a nice cut of inheritance as widow."

"The answer to 'Why kill Trimming,'" said Lancing. "I think one of the most astute ideas in the whole show was that Delafield was left alive to describe how he heard Trimming fall downstairs. If he'd stayed in his bed, or just bawled out of the window for help, so that he could have given evidence when help arrived, do you think the whole thing would have been accepted as accident?"

"Might have been," said Rivers, "and it wouldn't even have mattered if he'd said he was married to her—it wouldn't have brought her back to life. But getting back to this inheritance theme again. Did it cross your mind, while you were wondering if Miss Virgilia had been the witch wielding the broomstick, that she wasn't really a person who cared a great deal about money for herself? She had a frugal nature."

"And so—if she did it, whom did she do it for?"

Rivers nodded. "It's easy to be wise after the event, but didn't she do it to endow the son she had once disowned? The baby she 'let go'?"

Lancing nodded. "Yes... she'd better have left it alone."

"She built up a wonderful background," said Rivers. "Trimming was unbalanced (as indeed she was), Trimming fasted and got dizzy. Then the plasterer was a halfwit, who left his gear unsafe so that a board fell on her—when witnesses were in earshot to uphold the story. Trimming was illiterate. We still don't know if she was, but the suggestion explained why we found no writing matter in Trimming's room. And the clock was smashed to time things for us. Never was a more detailed or industrious murder." He paused, and then said slowly: "But I'm glad she finished it as she did. I should have hated to see her hanged—knowing everything. And Roy got what he deserved."

Lancing nodded. "Left her to do the dirty work originally while he was safe in France—and then tried to land Raven with the blame for killing Potts."

Rivers nodded and looked across at the covered way. "Dilapidations," he said slowly. "I hope the ground landlord pulls down that thing for a start. It reminds me of the way to an execution shed." And Lancing nodded as he heard the mortuary van draw up.

5

The conclusion of the case came when Peter Raven had recovered sufficiently to give his own explanations—most of which Rivers had pieced together from his own investigations into De Fraine's record.

"I knew Braithwaite pretty well in Germany," said Peter. "We were in Field Security together for some time. I won't go so far as to say that I didn't trust him, but I certainly didn't trust De Fraine, who was one of his friends. I always believed that De Fraine was a chap who would hunt with the hounds while running with the hares. I knew he looted—and sold his loot. And I believed he'd sell security information if he could get a price for it. But I didn't *know.* I forgot all about him when we came out of the army, and I didn't think of him again until I caught sight of him and Braithwaite in a pub together about a month ago. Then I saw them walking down Baker Street together."

"Wait a minute. Was the pub you saw them in the Blenheim, in St. John's Wood?"

"Yes. I happened to go in there for a drink, and I got the idea they were hatching something. You know the way we've all been 'security minded'? I took a fancy to finding out what De Fraine was doing, where he lived, and what he was up to with Braithwaite. You see, in his job as courier Braithwaite went to and from the continent. He could smuggle—or act as intermediary."

"Why not have reported your little ideas to security officers this side?" asked Rivers.

"Well, I'd nothing to go on," said Raven. "I'd been in the army with Braithwaite and we'd been shot at together, so to speak. If I'd turned some of our bloodhounds on to him, his life as a courier would have been short. Suspicion works that way—you should know. Anyway, I thought I'd mooch round and see if I could spot him with De Fraine again."

"In St. John's Wood?"

"Yes. Around where I'd seen him with Braithwaite. And it was only chance that I spotted De Fraine in that sports car in the Mall when I was going to meet Susan. I turned round and followed him; and I think the reason why I chased him so persistently was because he was so obviously determined to get away."

"He had his reasons," said Rivers, and Raven nodded what was obviously an aching head.

"Yes. And believe it or believe it not, it wasn't until I was actually chasing De Fraine that I remembered he was a fresco painter in civilian life, and that Braithwaite had worked with him decorating a wall in barracks in Germany. They plastered the wall as they painted."

"Yes," said Rivers. "Fresco painting can be defined as painting on wet lime plaster with pigments mixed with water and lime."

Peter nodded wearily. "I know. We were talking about it the first time Braithwaite butted in on the Trubys, when we were having tea at that art exhibition at Verulam House. Susan asked Roy if he painted, seeing he was Delafield's grandson, and he said, No. I said he'd done some fresco painting with De Fraine in Germany and that De Fraine was a jolly good painter—"

"Here, steady on," said Rivers. "You mean that you talked about a friend of Roy Braithwaite's doing fresco, and you knew what fresco implied, and Susan Truby was there and Jocelyn Truby was there, and they must both know how fresco painting is done—and yet not one of you mentioned the fact to me, not even when you knew I was hunting for a plasterer?"

"You said an old plasterer," said Raven crossly. His head ached, and he wished Rivers would go.

"Yes," said Rivers, who had the wits to perceive that a concussed patient had talked about enough. "But age can be imitated more easily than youth—a slouch, a shuffling walk, an open mouth, a white wig and plenty of plaster dust under an old hat; and Trimming was as blind as a bat, anyway. The plasterer was De Fraine—obliging his friend Braithwaite. That's why he knocked you over the head—going interfering where you'd no business."

"And serve me damn' well right, is what you mean," said Raven weakly.

"To my credit, I didn't say so," said Rivers. "Well, thanks for the explanation, and I'm sorry I've given you a worse headache."

As he went down the hospital steps, Rivers muttered to himself, "Fresco painting—and they all heard him say it; all of them…"

He was still muttering to himself when he saw Susan Truby, crossing the road to the hospital. He stopped to speak to her, because she looked desolate—and Rivers liked Susan.

"All right. You can go and see him; he's got a clean bill from me. But don't let him talk too much. He's still got a bad headache. Perhaps the sight of you will do it good," he added. "And, anyway, God bless you!"

Susan beamed. "You too!" she cried. "And thanks a lot."

"Thank you for nothing," murmured Rivers to himself as he crossed the road. Then he grinned. "They're cut out for one another, both completely haywire. Good luck to them."

ALSO AVAILABLE
BY THE SAME AUTHOR

Trouble is brewing for the Hoggetts and their friend Chief Inspector Macdonald in Lunesdale, deep in the Lancashire fell country. By the jagged cliffs and chilling depths of a secluded quarry pool, strange noises disturb the night, and after an architect surveying the area is nearly hoisted into the cold waters by an unseen assailant, suspicions of a cold current of crime running through the area become a matter for the police.

First published in 1949, this classic of Lake District crime fiction pairs Lorac's evocative depictions of her beloved Lunesdale with a twisting and intelligent puzzle for Chief Inspector Macdonald.

ALSO AVAILABLE
BY THE SAME AUTHOR

When a civil servant at the newly formed Ministry of Fine Arts is found crushed beneath a monstrous marble bust after dark, it appears to be the third instance in a string of fatal accidents at the department. Already disturbed by rumours of forgeries and irregularities in the Ministry's dealings, Minister Humphry David is soon faced with the possibility that among his colleagues is a murderer—though how the bust could have been made an instrument of death is a masterstroke of criminal devilment. Taking charge of the case, Inspector Julian Rivers of Scotland Yard enters a caustic world of fine art and civil service grievances to unveil a killer hiding in plain sight.

ALSO AVAILABLE
IN THE BRITISH LIBRARY
CRIME CLASSICS SERIES

Big Ben Strikes Eleven	DAVID MAGARSHACK
Death of an Author	E. C. R. LORAC
The Black Spectacles	JOHN DICKSON CARR
Death of a Bookseller	BERNARD J. FARMER
The Wheel Spins	ETHEL LINA WHITE
Someone from the Past	MARGOT BENNETT
Who Killed Father Christmas?	ED. MARTIN EDWARDS
Twice Round the Clock	BILLIE HOUSTON
The White Priory Murders	CARTER DICKSON
The Port of London Murders	JOSEPHINE BELL
Murder in the Basement	ANTHONY BERKELEY
Fear Stalks the Village	ETHEL LINA WHITE
The Cornish Coast Murder	JOHN BUDE
Suddenly at His Residence	CHRISTIANNA BRAND
The Edinburgh Mystery	ED. MARTIN EDWARDS
Checkmate to Murder	E. C. R. LORAC
The Spoilt Kill	MARY KELLY
Smallbone Deceased	MICHAEL GILBERT
The Story of Classic Crime in 100 Books	MARTIN EDWARDS
The Pocket Detective: 100+ Puzzles	KATE JACKSON
The Pocket Detective 2: 100+ More Puzzles	KATE JACKSON

Many of our titles are also available
in eBook, large print and audio editions